Forget
Me Not
Garden

Forget Me Not Garden

Anna Fischer

authorHOUSE®

AuthorHouse™ LLC
1663 Liberty Drive
Bloomington, IN 47403
www.authorhouse.com
Phone: 1-800-839-8640

Published by AuthorHouse 07/29/2014

ISBN: 978-1-4969-3091-0 (sc)
ISBN: 978-1-4969-3090-3 (e)

Library of Congress Control Number: 2014913574

CONTENTS

CHAPTER ONE

Sunset

The forget-me-not flower: such a small and delicate flower. Have you ever considered what it represents? It represents remembrance and love. In its frail petals, it holds our most cherished and precious memories. Even when someone dies, they can hear the small flower's whisper, "Fear not, for I will forget you not." And a person can rest in peace knowing that one's memories live on in a flower.

Emily and Edward

"Do you know what my favorite flower is, Ed?" Emily asked. The two of them were sitting on top of a hill overlooking the town. It was sunset, and Edward Mikes and Emily Thorn often came to there to watch it. There was a huge boulder that was perfect for the two of them to sit on. She was leaning against him, with her head tucked under his chin. Edward supported her slight weight easily. He had one arm wrapped around her, and he leaned back on the other.

"Of course I do," Edward replied, uneasy.

Emily waited expectantly. When he didn't answer again, she laughed and looked up at him. "Well, what is it, then, silly?"

"It's, uh, roses, right? Red roses."

Emily laughed again. "Wrong! But don't feel bad; I never told you. I love flowers, but of all of them my favorite is the forget-me-not."

"Why that one? It's so small. Figures though; you're small too." Edward laughed and hugged her closer, relieved she wasn't mad at him. The two of them had been sweethearts since they were fifteen, and both of them were now eighteen. They would be in the graduating class of May 1968. Neither of them had thought much of the future; they just knew they wanted each other in it. Edward had a part-time job at an auto repair shop. He figured he would just work there full-time after school. But Emily had talked about becoming a teacher or a nurse. It wasn't something they were too concerned with, because after high school, the world would be their oyster.

They were both attractive young people. Edward had curly, rich, brown hair and deep brown eyes. He was tall and strongly built. He liked to play football on his high school team, and he was one of the best. Emily had long, ash-blond hair that fell past her shoulders. She had dark blue eyes with just a splash of green in them. Emily had a feminine, willowy build. She was also tall, but still the top of her head only reached Edward's chin.

For some reason Emily had always been self-conscious about how she looked, worried that she was too plain. To Edward, she was easily the most beautiful woman in the town. After all, there were so many things about her that Edward found beautiful. Her skin was pale and creamy; her lips were pink and so kissable. She moved with a certain grace about her, almost like a flower moving to a breeze, and she was always quiet and reserved. She was also sweet as hell. Edward figured he had loved her as long as he had known her.

"I know they're small, and it's not just that they're pretty either."

"What?" Edward asked, having forgotten what they were talking about. He absently touched the ring he had given her for her sixteenth birthday. It was a simple ring, all he could afford at the time, but Emily insisted that she loved it. The ring had a golden band with a small sapphire stone on the top in the shape of a heart. Emily's birthday was December twentieth, and Edward thought that her birthday was a very important thing. He had wanted to get her something special for it. The ring sat on her right ring finger. They had decided it was a promise ring. She never took it off. It meant a lot to him to see her wear it, something from him.

"Forget-me-not flowers. The reason why I like them is because of what they represent. You know, memories. They're so small and quiet, but to me they represent the respect and love we feel for another. They're the flowers my dad put on my mom's grave, you know."

Ed did know, because he remembered when Emily's mom died. Emily had been twelve, and Edward had hugged her while she cried. They had always been friends, but at that moment they were more than that. He held her to him like he was afraid she would fall apart, and she clung to him like he was the only solid object in the world. And while she cried, "It hurts," he could only whisper over and over again, "I'm sorry. I'm so sorry, Em."

Even before they were a couple, they had shared a deep connection. Edward had been there for Emily when her mom died, and Emily had been there for Edward when his dad drank himself to death. Ed had been fourteen at the time. As a kid he had always been afraid for himself and his mother. He never knew what kind of mood his father would be in. He worried about keeping his mom safe, while she was doing the same for him. It had almost been a relief when his dad died. Still, Edward continued to worry that there was something he could have done to save his father. Even worse, he worried that someday he would grow up to be like him.

Edward was a serious boy, and after his dad died he tried to withdraw from everyone. Emily wouldn't let him. Once, she came up behind him and wrapped her arms around his waist, buried her face in his back, and whispered, "How much longer are you going to beat yourself up over this? You're not your dad, Edward. You will never be like him. So stop running away from me."

After that, Edward still was serious, but he was able to live again, as if Emily had brought him back. She was his breath of fresh air, and that was when he realized he loved her more than a friend and more than she would ever know.

"Edward, isn't the sunset pretty?" Emily asked. She had turned around and was leaning against his chest again.

To Edward, no sunset could ever compete with Emily. He did love the way the setting sun reflected off of her hair and turned it to gold. He could also appreciate how the fading sunlight made her white skin glow, and how her eyes widened in wonder at the sky's colors. So he hugged her closer and agreed, loving her scent. She always smelled like lavender and rain, and he inhaled deeply.

This was their favorite time of day. Of course he didn't mind holding her close while listening to the rain or even while watching the snow. Sometimes they came up here to watch the lightning in the distance or to see the snowflakes falling. Right now the weather was clear and cool, with dusk approaching on an October day. There were a lot of forest areas around Maple Valley, and the leaves on the trees were a mixture of red, orange, and yellow. They could see the mountains off in the distance, which added to the serenity and beauty.

"Maybe if anything ever happens to me, you could hold a forget-me-not and remember everything about me!" Emily laughed.

"Nothing's going to happen to you," Edward said, immediately trying to banish the thought. "And even if something did, what need would I have of flowers?"

Emily nodded with her head lying against his chest and Edward leaned down to kiss her on the head inhaling the sweet fragrance of her hair. She looked up at him with a serious expression. "I love you, Edward Mikes. Don't ever forget that."

"I love you too, Emily," Edward said gruffly and held her closer.

They walked back to town, her small hand in his larger, stronger one, but he was always careful not to hold too tight. "You know, the carnival got to town last night. It'd be sad if we didn't go," Emily said absently.

"Yeah, but we didn't miss anything. They were just setting up everything. We can go tomorrow."

"Tomorrow's Halloween."

"I know. Do you want to go? It'll be fun."

"Well, okay. It's a date!"

The carnival had been coming to Maple Valley during the week of Halloween for as long as they both could remember. It was a big carnival with rides, animals, shows, and games. They set up the carnival near the forest, by Cedar River.

As children, Emily and Edward had loved all the flashing lights against the chilly night sky. They'd watch the acts in a huge tent with the ringmaster, the lion tamer, and the clowns. Emily wasn't a fan of the clowns, but Edward would always yell, "I'll protect you, Em!" Growing up, the carnival was a fun and almost magical place. Now that they were young adults, it was a romantic place. Last year Ed had won Emily a huge teddy bear that Emily loved and kept in her room at home.

But the carnival also had a dark side, or at least that's what Edward's mother told him: "Stay away from the fortune and future tellers. They are liars and bad people." Carnivals were shady places, with tents that held cheats and freaks. Edward never gave much thought to them. He and Emily usually stayed in more open and inviting areas.

"I don't think we've ever gone right on Halloween. That'll be different," Emily said.

"It'll be fun. I'll pick you up at your house. Seven okay?"

"Yeah, it sounds good," Emily answered. They came up to Emily's house, Edward lived a few blocks away, but he always walked her home after they had been out together.

"Smells like Dad's got dinner ready," Emily said and made a face. Emily's father, David Thorn, was by far the worst cook in town. Of course, he never had to worry about cooking before his wife, Mary, died, but afterward he tried to keep up with housework. Emily often took over before too much damage had been done, but she loved her father all the more just for trying. "I'd better go see what I can salvage. Do you want to come in?" Emily asked teasingly as she took off the sport jacket Edward had loaned her while they were out and handed it back to him.

The smell of something burned filled Edward's nose, and he laughed as he took his jacket back. "Uh, I think I'll pass."

"Coward." She giggled, then sighed. "I'll see you tomorrow, Ed."

"Okay," he answered. He hugged her close and kissed her.

"I love you, Edward."

"Love you too, sweetheart," he said as he went to kiss her again. The porch light suddenly came on, and the two of them jumped back from another. The light meant that Emily's father was watching and wanted Emily to come in.

"He has the worst timing." Emily sighed and waved as she headed in.

Edward agreed as he held his hand up to wave too. He turned and started walking home, putting on his jacket and burying his hands in the pockets.

He dreamed of Emily that night. That wasn't unusual. Edward figured he'd been dreaming about Emily for years. But parts of this dream were different … and unsettling. They were lying together at their spot on top of the hill. Her head rested on his shoulder and her hand rested on his chest, right above his heart. His hand held hers as she curled up against him. They didn't say anything, just watched one another. Sometimes they did that; sometimes there was no need for words between them.

She was smiling up at him, her deep blue eyes staring into his. None of this seemed strange to Edward. Except the sky was different. Usually it was just at sunset in his dreams, when the light would make her shine next to him. But storm clouds loomed above them, flashes of lightning flickering across the sky. Thunder boomed in the distance. A storm was coming. He had to get Emily somewhere safe.

But Emily was suddenly different too, as he looked from the ominous sky to her face. Emily was always pale, but she was ghost white now, like the blood had been leached from her body. Her lips had lost their pinkness and were tinged with blue, as if she was cold. And her skin did feel cold, ice-cold; he could feel the iciness radiating from her hand resting on his chest. He tried to warm it with his own hand, but it was useless.

And her eyes … her blue eyes, so full of life, were distant somehow. She was still staring at him, but it was almost like she was staring through him, like she couldn't see him. Like her eyes saw nothing.

Rain started to fall, and he watched as raindrops splashed on her white skin. The storm was almost upon them, but Edward couldn't move. He stared at her and said, "Emily."

She focused on him for a moment and whispered, "Forget me not as I sleep."

There was suddenly a flash of lightning, and Emily was gone. Edward sat up, looking frantically around for her, but she had vanished. He stood, turning around, yelling her name.

"How far will you go to get her back?" a voice came. The rain started pouring down on him.

Edward jerked awake, sitting up in bed. The blankets were tangled around his legs. He was sweating and cold at the same time. He took several deep breaths, telling himself that it was just a dream, but his heart wouldn't stop racing. *Emily's safe. She's safe,* he told himself over and over again. That seemed to help, and he exhaled slowly.

Then he heard the rain. Edward looked out the window. *That's why I had the dream—I could hear the rain outside.* It was still early morning, and the rain looked like it would let up soon. He hoped so, anyway.

Edward lay back down in bed, his hand resting on his chest right above his heart. *Strange,* he thought. *It still feels cold there.*

Fate

She sat at her table alone. It was early morning, still dark out, and no one was awake yet. Even her pet barn owl slept on its peg. But she never slept much anyway. A lone candle burned beside her so she could see.

She owned her very own trailer, and her tent was outside. She was glad she had listened to her gut and put all her belongings in the trailer before it rained—belongings being her table, her cards, and her crystal ball.

It was just a lie, what the cards said. She knew a reality that was much worse. What good were cards? It was all for show.

It also hurt like hell, what she did for a living. Telling a future of love and hope to young couples and seeing them together. But it was worth it, because soon …

She smiled softly and took out the locket that rested between her breasts. It was a beautiful gold locket in the shape of a heart, with roses imprinted on it. She opened it and stared at the picture of the man she loved with all her heart. She had done it so many times, she'd lost count, but she never wanted to forget what he looked like. He was the most important thing in her world—and out of her world.

Her smile faltered. A tear slid down her lovely, pale cheek as she read the words next to his picture: *Love You Forever, Fate*. Simple words, but they meant everything to her.

She closed her eyes and let another tear fall. She was so close. Maybe it hurt most at this time of the year. And God, did it hurt right now, when she was remembering and still alone. "I miss you," she whispered.

A slight stirring in the air brushed across her face. *Soon we'll be together again.* She heard the faint, masculine voice and her heart skipped a beat, because it was his voice. It was so close to the time that she could feel his presence more strongly. Sometimes she could sense him other days too. Although it was faint, she knew he was standing by her side.

He was right, too. She let herself smile again, shut her locket, and let it fall back to rest by her heart, her ever-beating heart. *Soon.* She whispered it in her head, and her heart sighed with longing. This time would be different though. Change was in the air, and she could feel it.

Grim Reaper

He inhaled slowly and then exhaled through his nose. The air was different here on his side; it was always heavy and thick, like it was going to rain. It was always night here too, but without any moon or stars. He could see the other side, but it was cast in a twilight glow to him. He would never be a part of the sun again.

He himself was only a shadowy part of the person he used to be. He supposed he more or less looked the same as he had when he was alive, except his skin was so pale as to be almost transparent, and he wore a dark robe from his neck to his black boots. He carried a scythe with him at all times, a massive rod with a wicked sharp blade, but he barely noticed its weight. He leaned against a tree for a spell and observed the progress his charges were making. He was the Grim Reaper. Death. He watched over the dead constantly, guiding them to where their souls would rest for eternity.

He could move anywhere he wanted in his shadowy world at any time. He reaped and then guarded the souls as they traveled to where they needed to go. They all traveled on the main path at first. After a while, the path split into two ways. Some souls went north above the highest mountains and beyond the clouds, and some went south, beneath the scorching deserts and melting lava. One should never want to go south.

His job was without rest, but he never required rest. Time passed without meaning to him or the souls he watched over. Most of the time they weren't even aware of his presence. Sometimes he merely directed them with a slight wave of his hand. It was a never-ending job, but it was the price he had to pay.

He closed his eyes for a moment and sighed again. Fate. She was sad; he could feel it. He could sense her longing for him, longing to close her eyes and rest with him. It was all he wanted as well.

He could watch over her, although she was rarely able to tell if he was near. Sometimes she could. To see her alive, to see her breathing in real air, was enough for him, but he knew she missed him. And God, did he miss her too, at all times, so much so that his never-beating heart would ache as well.

He suddenly heard "I miss you," and he could feel her touching the locket that he gave her so many years ago.

My Fate, she's calling me, he thought. So he called on the night wind he had command over and gave her a message. Sometimes they could do that—not often, but sometimes she was that much attuned to his soul. She heard his message and smiled, and he felt relief that she wasn't hurting. "Soon," he heard her sigh.

Yes, soon they would be together again. For one night a year, he could hold her in his arms, smell her hair, and feel the warmth of her skin. He would be among the living, but only for one night. Only she could see him, but that was enough for him. She was the only thing that mattered to him.

Somewhere over the endless time he had spent in the shadow world, he felt that he had lost all his human self. He liked to think that everything—his feelings and emotions, his humanity—rested in her. It was almost hard coming back once a year. It had hurt the first time he inhaled the air in the living world. But then she would be in his arms, and he would remember what it was like to be in her world again, even though he would always be dead.

He was brought back to the present when a soul tripped and fell. It was the soul of a young child, around the age of four. The soul started to cry as it sat on the ground. He sighed but immediately straightened from the tree he was leaning against and walked over. Usually the souls walked without much thought or emotion, but occasionally they could become upset or restless, mostly over the smallest things. He made a straight path for it, the other souls automatically moving out of his way, for they became aware he was one they answered to.

He made it to the soul and bent down on one knee beside it. "You are fine. You just tripped." He picked the soul up, brushed it off, and put it back on its feet. The soul was that of a little girl. He recognized her of course; he could name every soul he reaped, and also see the time when they were alive. This little one had died from drowning. He was the first thing she saw as he reached a hand out to her to pull her from the water. She was going due north to the clouds and light.

She stared up and him and murmured, "I fell."

She was referring to now and to how she died when she fell into the river. "Yes," he answered, "but you are fine now."

"Mommy," she whispered.

"Your mother isn't coming yet, but someday soon you will be together again. Your grandmother is waiting for you, little one. It's time to join her."

She surprised him by taking his hand in hers and smiling. A rare gesture, but she was young and just recently reaped. She must still be holding human thoughts in her head. He sat there for a moment and let her hold his hand, not in any hurry. Her cheerful smile suddenly vanished, and a thoughtful expression took its place.

"Sad." She voiced the concern and pointed at him. He was surprised that she could sense what he felt, but then she always had been an observant and attentive child. Also very sweet, but it was time for her to continue on her way.

"All right, little one. It's time to move," he said gruffly. She nodded and started to walk again. He followed her for a bit to make sure she was steady, decided she was, and then moved off of the path to stand beside it. He watched her progress to make sure she continued smoothly, and then walked to another tree and leaned against it.

Sad? Yes, he supposed that was a word to describe him. But soon he would see Fate again. The day was almost here, but there was something that bothered him. Besides reaping and guarding the path, there was one other job he attended to. It was the reason he was here, the reason he had come to be who he was now. The gate to the garden was open.

Demon

He sat hunched over an old, worn table, mumbling to himself. He was such a painfully skinny man that his vertebrae were easily seen. Even through his ratty and dirty shirt, his spine stuck out. There was a deck of playing cards sitting on the table, but his attention was only focused on one. This one was the only one that mattered to him. "No good, no good," he muttered again and again as he leaned over it, his tangled, greasy hair falling over the card. "Sin, sin, my name means sin," he prattled on. "No chance of salvation. Not for me."

He talked as though his head were full of demons, but it wasn't. There was just him in his head, and that alone was madness. And his name did mean sin; his very being was sin. In fact there were seven of them. They even had a title: the Seven Deadly Sins.

He and his siblings didn't feel the need to keep in touch often, and he was glad for that because he hated being around his brothers and sister. Out of all of them, he feared that he was most pathetic. He didn't have Pride's arrogance or Wrath's ferocity, and right now he was pretty sure that Greed was living it up in a palace or someplace. He didn't have Lust's beauty that led many a man away from their wives. Hell, even his siblings agreed that he was pathetic, as Pride once said with disdain some two hundred years ago or so. Hell? That was funny to him, and he chuckled. Hell existed in his head.

Looking at him, one would never have been able to guess he was a demon. That being said, one would also have wanted to keep one's distance from him. He was an unsavory-looking man with long, greasy brown hair and an unsteady gait, and he was too skinny to be normal. His eyes were green with yellow mixed in, and they were always lit up feverishly. He shifted around nervously, as if afraid something was coming for him … and maybe something was. His skin was so sun bleached that it looked permanently burned. He had surprisingly white teeth, but they were pointed. He was the type of man people would avoid, the type that didn't fit in. Except here.

He fitted in just fine here at the carnival, with all the other dark freaks in the outer tents. He wasn't here all the time. It was just a place he came every once in a while to hang his hat. And something was coming. He could feel it, the anxiety making his skin crawl and his fingers twitch. This was something important to him, that made him want. And he wanted everything everyone else had.

"My name means jealousy. Pathetic. Pathetic Envy," he spat. Demon Envy, one of the Seven Deadly Sins. Envy desired what everyone else had. He wanted to have goals and dreams, to laugh and to know the joy of being a human being. How pathetic to be jealous of the very beings he tried to condemn. Being human was dangerous—they were such fragile and simple things. Fleeting too, for a human life could easily be snuffed out like the flame of a candle. And Envy would know. How many lives had he taken over the centuries and sent below? Too many to count. None of his siblings understood why he longed to have what humans had. Not even Envy understood, and it added to the never-ending despair he felt in the core of his being.

There was one thing he wanted above all others. He wanted love. Such a simple word, but such a powerful emotion when it was truly meant. He saw hundreds of different loves expressed in hundreds of different ways, and he yearned and craved for it. How could he not want love? Wasn't love the very reason these simple and foolish mortals had even the slightest chance of salvation from one higher than all of them? What love could a demon ever hope to have?

But, as he had thought earlier, human beings were easily breakable. Whatever Envy wanted and couldn't have, he pursued. He wouldn't rest until he tore that possession out of the owner's hands and destroyed the precious object in front of his horrified eyes.

CHAPTER TWO

The Carnival

Emily and Edward

*E*dward still felt groggy when he got up later that morning. The rain had stopped, but it was cloudy out. He stood at his bathroom sink and ran a hand through his rumpled brown hair and splashed cold water on his face to wake himself up. Then he looked at himself in the mirror. For some reason he felt like he had aged years in his sleep, but he looked the same and didn't know what else he had expected.

Emily. That was the first thing that popped in his head when he woke up, the first face he saw. He didn't understand why he felt this concern about her safety. Edward knew she was safe at home right now. Her old man, Dave, would blow the head off of anyone who tried to hurt her, under his roof or anyplace else. Yet he felt this strange anxiety, a sense of danger.

He placed his hand over his heart, over the same spot he had dreamed that Emily placed her hand last night. He could feel his heart beating steadily. A bit fast, he supposed, with all this anxiety, and the spot didn't feel cold like he would have sworn it had last night. Emily's hand had been so cold in his dream, and he couldn't warm it.

He looked at his face in the mirror. He was surprised to see a determined look in his eyes. He would protect Emily no matter what.

"Aw, I'm losing it." Edward groaned and ran his hand down his face. "Shake it off already!" He straightened, went back to his room, and got dressed in a pair of jeans and a red T-shirt. He threw his jersey on too, the one with the picture of a bear on it—their Tahoma High School mascot. He added socks and his favorite pair of tennis shoes and he was ready to go.

Edward went to leave his bedroom, but hesitated at the door. A sudden wave of sadness filled him, and he didn't know why. His room looked the same as always. His eyes scanned his walls, his bed, and finally the picture resting on his nightstand. It was a picture of him and Emily next sitting next to each other, grinning at the camera. They were celebrating Edward's seventeenth birthday at his house, and his mom had snapped the picture. His arm was around Emily's shoulders.

Edward had seen this picture hundreds of times before. Why was he sad now? Like he wouldn't see it or his room again?

"Losing it!" he said out loud. He turned and headed downstairs to the smell of bacon and pancakes. His mom, Sarah Mikes, smiled at him from the stove.

"Well, good morning, honey." She beamed, her long brown hair pulled back from her face and her warm brown eyes shining at him.

"Morning, Mom," Edward said and started getting the dishes out to set the table for two. "Breakfast smells good."

"Good. It'll be ready in a minute. Happy Halloween, by the way."

"Uh, you too."

"I love Halloween, mostly because I got to dress you up in the cutest costumes and take you all over town."

"Ugh, Mom. That was a long time ago."

"I know, but you always had such a good time, especially when Emily started coming with us. You were so sweet to her. No matter what, you always made sure Emily had more candy than you at the end. Even then, you had a thing for her. It was so adorable!"

"Okay, Mom. That's enough remembering." Edward groaned, finished setting the table, and sat down. His mother chuckled and brought over a plate of pancakes. Edward served himself three, poured maple syrup all over, and chowed down. He loved his mom's cooking, and Sarah loved to cook. They made an equal trade because Edward always cleaned up after, even when his mom told him he didn't have to.

"My little responsible man," she would say sadly. But Edward worried that she worked too hard, and he tried to make up for it by doing chores around the house. His mother was a nurse. Edward helped out with the bills with his part-time job at the auto repair shop. He knew his mom felt guilty, thinking that he was somehow missing out on life, but he never wanted to see his mother struggling to make ends meet for the both of them.

"So, got any plans for tonight?" Sarah asked as she sat down at the table with the bacon.

"Emily and I are going to hang out at the carnival today."

"Oh, that will be fun. That brings back memories too. We always tried to go when you were little. We never went on Halloween though. That's a change."

"Yeah. Did you need me for anything?"

"No. I don't work tonight, so I'll stay home and hand out candy to the trick or treaters. That'll be fun. I love seeing all the children dressed up."

"Yeah, that sounds like lots of fun."

His mom chuckled and then her face turned serious. "There was something I wanted to talk to you about."

Edward froze, fork frozen in midair. "Uh-oh."

"It's nothing bad, silly. Just something I wanted to ask," She waited until he slowly started eating again, eyes suspicious, before she said, "So you and Emily are a pretty serious couple now. You've been dating for a couple of years, and you've known each other much longer than that."

"Oh, Mom! You're not going to try and have *the talk* with me again, are you?" Edward asked, horrified.

"No, no." She waved the question aside. "I know you're being very responsible and I'm proud of you, but that's not it." Edward sighed in relief. Then his mom continued, "So what are your plans? Are you two thinking about marriage?"

Edward was suddenly serious. He was relieved that they were no longer having *the talk*, and the truth was he never thought of life without Emily being in it. But now that the conversation had turned into the word *marriage*, it felt strange. Strange but also right in a way.

Edward had always figured that he and Emily would get married someday, but everything was clear to him now that his mother asked. He looked at his mom across the table. She had never wanted anything but the best for him in life. He finally answered, surprised at how easily the words came together. "I don't want to be without Emily. I want her in my life always. I'm not sure when for sure, but I do plan on asking her to marry me someday."

Edward was shocked when his mom's eyes suddenly filled with tears, but she smiled, "Oh, Edward, always my little adult. I thought you would either shrug the question away or you would get embarrassed and groan something like *Mom* at me. I was counting on that, and here you give me this all mature answer."

"Um, sorry?" Edward answered, not sure what to say.

"Don't be. I just want you to know how very proud I am of you, Edward."

"Thanks, Mom," Edward said, serious again.

Sarah sighed and then got up from the table. "Well, I guess I might as well give this to you now, since you're so grown-up."

Finished with breakfast, Edward pulled back from the table to and stood up. Sarah dug in her apron pocket and pulled out a little wooden box. "I would have waited to give this to you, but now I can see it's okay to give it to you now. Don't worry. I didn't spend any money on it. This has been in the family for near a century. It once belonged to my great-grandmother."

Sarah opened the box and Edward saw the ring. It was old-fashioned but still pretty. It had a gold band, and on top sat a simple white pearl with diamonds around it forming the shape of a flower. It was utterly feminine, and it must have been worth a lot.

Sarah continued, "This is your great-great-grandmother Marie's wedding ring. From what I remember hearing about her history, her husband was quite well off, and Marie had a fondness for pearls. I think she had a pearl necklace too, but I have no idea where that ended up. It's a shame. But I want you to have this for Emily. I love Emily like she was my daughter, and the two of you … sort of just belong together. I've watched you grow from childhood friends to a young adult couple. I've seen how the two of you look at each other. You're meant to be together; it's as simple as that. I know that you will be happy together. That's what I want for you, Edward. That's always what I wanted for you. Live life and be happy. Do that for me, and consider this a gift from me. Wedding rings are expensive, and this one will do just fine. It suits her. Give this to her when you're ready. Okay?" Sarah finished with a smile and a tear running down her cheek.

Edward didn't know what to say. He felt the lump in his throat and cleared it, and tried to ignore the sudden emotions he felt. Crying wasn't his thing—at least, it wasn't something he did. He hugged his mom if she cried when his dad took anger out on him or his mom. He hugged Emily when she cried. But Edward wouldn't.

He wiped Sarah's tear away with his thumb, wrapped one arm around her shoulders, and hugged her to him. He had to lean down to hug her—he was taller than she was—and Sarah leaned up, kissed him on his cheek, and hugged him back. Edward sighed; his mom always worried too much about him.

"I love you, Edward."

"I love you too, Mom," Edward answered. He straightened and took the box from her hand, tucking it carefully into his pocket. "Thank you for the gift. It's beautiful, and Emily will love it when I give it to her someday. Really, Mom, thanks. For everything."

"What are moms for? Let me clean up. I need something to distract me from all these emotions."

Edward grinned but still helped clean the table. When Sarah was at the sink washing the dishes, he thanked her for breakfast and started to head out.

"Edward?"

"Yes?" Edward asked as he turned back around to her.

Sarah was still smiling but now looked slightly uneasy. She finally answered, "You two have fun but be careful. Remember, parts of the carnival have a darker side to them. They shouldn't be messed with. Stay clear, okay?"

Edward rolled his eyes but answered, "Yeah, Mom, we will. Bye."

"Bye, Edward," Sarah whispered and turned back to the sink, hearing Edward leave but not wanting to see him go. She didn't know why another tear rolled down her cheek.

Edward got into his old Dodge pickup truck. Actually it had belonged to his dad, but when the man died, Sarah thought Edward should have it when he was old enough. Sarah preferred a car. It was a big truck and it was red. Edward was proud of it. He kept it in good shape and clean.

He turned the ignition and headed for Emily's house. He knew she would already be awake and have cooked breakfast for David, probably so she wouldn't have to wake to the smell of something burning. David could fry bacon— that was about it.

Emily's house wasn't far from Edward's, and he would have walked if they weren't going to the carnival out by Cedar River. Edward was looking forward to spending the day with Emily. They would have a lot of fun at the carnival. And …

His hand found the little wooden box with the ring in it. Probably not tonight, but he was truly grateful to his mother for giving this to him. Someday, he would propose to Emily. Of one thing he was sure: Edward wanted Emily in his life.

He pulled up in front of Emily's house and got out of his truck. He took a quick look at himself in the reflection of his window to make sure he looked presentable. He wanted not only to look good for Emily, but also for her father. Old Dave wasn't easy to impress, but it was a good idea to at least try. The last thing he wanted to hear was Old Dave telling Emily to stay away from the "bad boy with the rag clothes."

Edward figured he looked okay. He ran his hands through his brown hair. He walked up to the front door, calmly knocked, and waited patiently, careful not to slouch or put his hands in his pockets. Old Dave would watch him from the window before finally opening the door, always inspecting him. He inspected Edward when they were face-to-face too, but he had to be more discreet about it.

Sure enough, out of the corner of his eye, Edward saw the curtain on the front window flutter. He straightened even more, his hands resting patiently by his sides. Finally the curtain fluttered again and the door opened.

"Hello, Mr. Thorn," Edward greeted the older man politely. "How are you doing today?"

"Edward." David nodded and motioned him in. "Fine, and you?"

"Fine."

"Good, good," David muttered and stepped aside as Edward came in. "How's Sarah?"

"She's fine, thank you."

"Good," David answered. "How's work?"

"Fine for the both of us. Can't complain."

"Good."

They stood there awkwardly for a moment. Mr. Thorn wasn't much for words, and half the time Edward had no idea what to talk about with him anyway.

Old Dave was a damn intimidating man to be around. Not only was he a policeman, but he was a big, burly man with what seemed a permanent scowl on his face. He had the same ash-blond hair as Emily, but it was graying. He had sharp blue eyes that didn't miss anything. Edward did like him though, because although he was gruff, he was a fair man, and he loved his daughter more than anything.

Finally David murmured, "Uh, Emily's getting ready. Should be here in a bit." He sounded hopeful. Edward hoped so too.

Suddenly a laughing voice called down the stairs, "My two chatterboxes sure sound like they're having a good time. How will I be able to get a word in edgewise?"

Both men visibly relaxed when they heard Emily's voice and then her footsteps on the stairs. They turned to see her smiling down at them as she walked. Edward sighed when he saw her. She always had that effect on him. Like he could relax when he hadn't known he was slightly tense, or like he could breathe easier when he hadn't realized that he wasn't.

Emily made it down the stairs and smiled up at him. "Hi, Edward."

"Hi, Emily. You look nice." And she did. She was dressed in a flared, long-sleeved white dress that ended right at her knees, with lacing on the bodice and sleeves. She also wore her favorite pair of brown boots. Her hair was down and flowed around her shoulders as she walked over to him. She looked beautiful.

"Thanks," Emily said. David cleared his throat. Emily turned to her father and said in a mock-stern voice, "I hope you've been nice to my boyfriend, Dad."

But David took her seriously and said defensively, "He's still here, isn't he? Edward, we had a nice talk, didn't we?"

"Yes, sir, Mr. Thorn," Edward answered dutifully.

"Relax, Dad. I was just kidding. I know you were on your good behavior." Emily laughed and gave him a quick kiss on the cheek. David cleared his throat again, but couldn't help the smile.

"Bye, Dad. See you later tonight," Emily called as she tried to push Edward to the front door. Edward opened the door for her.

"You kids have fun."

"Yeah, Dad."

"Be careful, you hear?"

"Yeah, Dad."

They were almost out when David cleared his throat a third time. "Edward?"

Edward immediately stopped, despite Emily trying to pull him out the door, and turned back. "Yes, Mr. Thorn?"

Old Dave was staring right at him, so Edward straightened his back again and looked right back with a serious expression. David must have approved of that because he nodded. "You take good care of my daughter. Hear me?"

"Yes, sir," Edward replied seriously. "I'll keep her safe and bring her back home to you."

"Holding you to that."

"Don't worry. I'm a man of my word."

"I know you are, son."

Edward froze. Son? Old Dave had called him son? That had never happened before. Did it mean that Edward had finally won Emily's father's approval?

Emily must have heard that and wondered the same thing, because she stopped pulling Edward's arm and raised her eyebrows.

David didn't give them time to really think about it before he was shooing them out the door. "All right, all right. Day's not getting any younger. You two have fun." And he shut the door behind them.

Emily smiled and took Edward's hand again. She waited until they were almost to his truck before she whispered with a laugh, "Son?"

Edward grinned and shrugged. "I don't know."

"Guess you finally won him over."

"Guess so."

"I'm glad, so I can do this." She stopped at the truck and gave him a quick kiss on the cheek.

Both of them saw the curtain flutter. Edward quickly opened the passenger side the truck and murmured, "Don't push our luck." He helped her into the seat.

"Just an experiment."

"And I'm the guinea pig? He could come right out and arrest me."

"Nah, he wouldn't do that. He'd probably just shoot you to save time."

"Oh, gee, I sure would hate to be a burden on your old man. Guess you don't need me anymore," Edward finished as he got into the driver's seat.

She surprised him by taking his hand. He looked at her. She was still smiling, but she answered seriously, "I need you, Edward. Always."

"I need you too," he replied.

She gave him a quick kiss, on the lips this time. Inches from his face, she whispered, "I'm really glad to see you."

"I'm glad to see you too. Now let's get out of here before I kiss you back and your dad really does come out here. You think you're kidding, but I'm not so sure that he wouldn't try and shoot me."

They listened to the radio on the short drive to the carnival. "Piece of My Heart" by Big Brother and the Holding Company came on, and Emily felt the need to sing along to the lyrics. "Take it! Take another little piece of my heart, now, baby!" she sang, her lovely soprano voice not fitting in with the band's yelling. She added little dance moves, and Edward couldn't help laughing—which Emily intended for him to do. Around other people, Emily was much more reserved and composed, as was Edward. But when it was just the two of them, they could let other sides of themselves show. Emily did have a very funny side to her, and she always said that he was too serious.

When "Magic Carpet Ride" by Steppenwolf started, Edward joined in a couple of times, but he let Emily do the dancing bit. At one point Emily looked right at him, smiled, and took his hand, and Edward's heart felt like it skipped a beat. Looking at this bright, beautiful, and compassionate woman and knowing she was his was hard for him to understand. He just knew he was honored, and he held her hand in his.

The sun was high in the sky when Edward opened the passenger door and helped Emily climb out of the truck. The day was clear, with the faint scent of rain still in the air. The sun's rays shone through the autumn leaves still on the trees. Edward had found a parking spot next to a friend's car. The water in the Cedar River was running high from last night's rain.

The carnival was up and going, and it looked like a good group of people were already there enjoying themselves. Emily barely gave Edward enough time to lock his truck before she was pulling him along in her wake.

At first they walked around for a bit, enjoying watching people and remembering where everything was. They'd been coming here just about every year, but it was always fun to remember the old times. "Remember when Jamie threw up on the Tilt-a-Whirl when we were ten? It got in Rebecca's hair and she screamed and wouldn't talk to Jamie for the rest of the day!" Emily asked with a laugh.

"Yeah. Beauty Queen Rebecca looked like she wanted to murder someone that day. Probably Jamie." Edward chuckled.

"I told her that she was too much of a lightweight to get on. Remember how angry she got at me and said, 'I am not.

I'll show you!'?" Emily mimicked putting her hands on her hips and tossing her hair over her shoulders. That was Jamie, always believing she was right and easy to offend. To be honest, Jamie was pain in the ass. But she was a friend, or so Emily said to him the day of said accident. Emily had held back Jamie's hair as she went for round two of vomiting.

"Hey guys! Fancy meeting you two here. You going on the Tilt-a-Whirl?"

Emily and Edward turned to see two of their classmates, Joshua and Rose, standing behind them. Rose was the one who had asked them.

"Oh, hey," Emily said with a smile. "Yeah, we'll go. Right, Edward?"

"Sure," Edward answered.

"Oh, dudes, remember that day when Jamie puked her guts out and it got in Becky's hair? That was hilarious!" Joshua started laughing. Josh was on the football team with Edward, and the two of them were good friends. Josh was loud and loved a good time. He was shorter than Edward, but stockier. Josh loved nothing more than using that build to knock the other team's players down.

Josh and Rose were sort of a couple. Their personalities certainly clashed though. Where Josh was loud and forceful, Rose was polite and very shy. She was the quietest girl in their class, although everyone liked her. Rose was dainty and pretty, with pale blond hair and light green eyes. Josh was head over heels for her, and to his credit he really did try to impress her by acting calmer.

Even now he stopped laughing and quickly looked down at Rose to make sure she thought the memory was as funny as he did. But Rose loved Josh too, and had a very accepting nature. Joshua didn't need to worry as much as he did, but he didn't know for sure how to act around her. They've been dating for about a month. Edward knew Joshua had wanted to ask Rose out for forever. It certainly had seemed to take that long. It drove Edward crazy when all Joshua talked about was Rose. But then Edward realized he had probably done the same thing about Emily before he got the nerve to ask her out.

To Josh's relief, Rose smiled and said quietly, "Oh yeah, that was funny. Rebecca was so mad."

"We were just talking about that!" Emily laughed.

"Neither one of them would ever forgive us if they knew we were talking about it." Edward grinned, not concerned at all by the thought.

"Ah, they always were crybabies. Might as well get a few laughs at their expenses." Joshua shrugged and then cast another worried look down at Rose, afraid he had offended her.

Rose laughed and took Josh's hand, "Stop worrying so much, Josh. You're funny and I'm having a good time. Don't be afraid to say things in front of me. Let's go on the ride."

Joshua relaxed again and said with a sheepish grin, "Okay. You two lovebirds coming or what?"

"Yeah we're coming," Edward answered for them. "And who are you calling lovebirds, Mr. Smooth?"

Joshua shoved him with his free hand but didn't let go of Rose's hand as they walked up to the ride.

The four of them went on some rides and then decided to eat a late lunch at one of the vendors. While Emily and Rose found somewhere to sit, Joshua and Edward bought the food. Edward ordered their hot dogs, chips, and sodas.

Edward already knew what Emily's favorite soda was—Dr Pepper—and he ordered a Mountain Dew for himself.

Suddenly he heard a groan from Joshua. "Oh, dude, I don't know what Rose wants to drink!"

"So ask her."

"That wouldn't look good. Here you just order everything for your girl, and I don't even know for sure what mine wants. She'll think I don't know anything about her! She'll dump me!"

"Oh, for God's sake! Get a grip, Josh. You're bugging the hell out of me."

"Oh, yeah? What do you think you were like when you first started going out with Emily. It was always, 'Do you think she'll like this?' or 'Isn't she just beautiful?' Which she is, but I'm trying to get Rose to like me. Help a brother out, man!"

"She already likes you, Josh. You're worrying too much." Edward turned, walked over to where the girls were sitting under a tree, and asked Rose what she wanted to drink. Rose smiled and Emily just laughed. Rose answered and Edward nodded. He walked back to Josh, who had turned a bright red. Edward said, "She wants a lemonade. And extra mustard on her hot dog. And for you to chill out."

"Right." Joshua sighed, then smiled. "Thanks, man."

"No problem. They're hungry; let's go."

"Okay." They paid and then walked back to Emily and Rose.

Emily accepted her soda, took a drink, and kissed Edward on the cheek. "Thanks, Edward."

"Sure thing," Edward answered.

Rose shyly took her lemonade from Joshua and thanked him too. She didn't kiss him, but when he sat down next to her, she leaned against his shoulder while they ate.

"Oh, hey, did you guys hear about the fortune-teller? They say she's for real," Joshua asked Emily and Edward.

"No, I haven't heard of a fortune-teller. What's his name?" Emily asked.

"*Her* name is Fate. Her tent's on the outskirts of the carnival, and she will see people later this evening. You know, after all the families go home. Her tent has a sign in front of it that says 'Know Your Fate.' Pretty cool, right?"

Edward snorted. "If you believe that kind of stuff."

"I'm not saying I believe in that crap, smart-ass. Oh, sorry," Josh said, quickly glancing down at Rose again.

She just smiled and said, "I don't believe in it either, but it's interesting. Wouldn't it be cool if she could actually tell our fortunes? Like who our true love is—or something like that," Rose finished with a blush. Joshua grinned broadly.

"I already know that," Edward said without any doubt, looking down at Emily. She smiled sweetly up at him.

"I think I have an idea too," Josh said, putting his arm around Rose's shoulders. Her blush deepened, but she laid her head down on his shoulder.

"Well, it's about time, you two," Emily joked. But seeing that Rose was almost bright red, she changed the subject back to what they had been talking about. "I don't believe in fortune-tellers or luck or anything like that. But it's just for fun, right?"

"Right," Edward agreed.

They finished eating. Edward and Josh decided to be competitive and tried to best each other at darts. Emily just rolled her eyes at Rose as they walked to the vendor, the men shoving each other on the way, but the girls waited. Finally Edward claimed he had popped the most balloons. Joshua disagreed, but both of them had won their dates stuffed animals.

Afterward they went into the center tent to watch the performers. They took their seats on the benches while the ringmaster announced with great enthusiasm all of what the performers would show. Emily loved the acrobats flying in the air. The last performance was a group of clowns driving away in a tiny car. The ringmaster bowed low to the audience, and they got up to leave.

On the way out, Edward bumped into someone. He turned and saw who it was: a beautiful young woman with raven-black hair that fell to her midback and a small, slender body. Her eyes were a deep emerald green, and she was very pale with slight, dark bruises under her eyes. Like she needed to get a good night's sleep. She was a beautiful lady, but to Edward no one could compete with Emily.

He apologized to her. She looked alarmed, and for a moment he thought she wanted to say something to him. But the crowd was pushing him away, and he lost sight of her. He thought about going back, but decided that it wasn't necessary. He had apologized, after all.

They ran into a few more of their classmates, and as a group they decided to get on the Ferris wheel. The sun was getting lower, and the sight of the sunset and the mountains was beautiful.

Emily and Edward sat next to each other, Emily wearing Edward's sport jacket, and waited until they were the ones at the top. They sat there for a while and stared out at the view, his arm around her shoulders.

"Isn't this pretty?" Emily said. "I know we've seen a lot of sunsets together, but I love this one. It's special somehow, but I can't quite figure out why."

"Every sunset with you is important to me," Edward answered, watching the sunset reflect in her eyes.

She turned to smile at him. "I love you, Edward. Forever."

"I love you too. More than you'll ever know." He kissed her. She wrapped her arms around his neck. They could have stayed like that forever.

Eventually they got off. They noticed that in a small clearing amid carnival, their classmates had gathered, and some of the couples were dancing. Music was playing on speakers throughout the carnival, and their classmates were taking advantage of it.

Emily smiled up at Edward and pulled him over to them. Edward immediately took Emily in his arms. They started dancing just as "Nights in White Satin" by the Moody Blues came on. They saw Josh taking Rose in his arms as they joined in.

Emily and Edward swayed in time with the music. Emily's eyes closed as she laid her head against Edward's chest. Edward inhaled the lavender-rain scent of her hair and was beyond a doubt content.

"I don't want today to end," Emily murmured against his shoulder.

Edward couldn't have agreed more. They both could have stayed like that forever.

Demon

He had been watching them for a while now. The two of them together, so happy, so in love. So vulnerable. Envy saw how the girl looked up at the boy with absolute love in her eyes, and he felt such jealousy and rage that he could have ripped something apart with his bare hands. Or someone. He had before.

What had that boy ever done to deserve the pure love radiating off of the beautiful young girl? Love was something Envy would never have. Who could ever love something as loathsome as him?

Jealousy was something Envy had lived with for all of his life, but it had been a long time since he felt this white, blinding rage. This savage instinct to tear the two of them apart.

None of his emotions showed on his face though. He must have looked completely calm, as no people indicated they were alarmed by him. No unearthly, animal snarls were coming from his mouth, so that was good. To the regular person, he was just another vendor, calmly ambling around and leaning against the tent poles. So what if his appearance was strange? They were at a carnival, after all.

Demon Envy continued to watch as he flicked a card back and forth in his hand. The card danced in his fingers with hardly a movement. Finally he tore his eyes from the couple long enough to glance down at the card. The ace of spades was showing. The symbol of death. And Demon Envy grinned.

CHAPTER THREE

Twenty-One

Emily and Edward

The sun had sunk beneath the mountains and stars started appearing. A pale moon hung in the sky, and the air smelled like autumn and the carnival. It was a beautiful Halloween night.

Families with kids in hand started to head to their cars. Their group of classmates slowly drifted away as well as the evening wore on. Even Rose and Joshua called out a good-night as they walked hand in hand to Josh's car. But Emily joked that they probably weren't heading home just yet. The two of them strolled around the carnival, enjoying the night, neither of them in any hurry.

After a while, Emily sighed. "It's getting late. My dad will start freaking out."

"Yeah, I know," Edward agreed. "Are you ready to leave?"

"I guess. It was fun tonight though. We'll have to remember this for next year."

"Sure. I'd like to do it again too."

With Emily's hand in his, they headed toward his truck. They were almost to the carnival's gates when they heard a low voice coming from the shadows. "Nice night, isn't it? Perfect for a young couple to be out together."

The two of them turned to see a man leaning against one of the tent poles. It was too dark to see him clearly, but they saw part of his face when he lit up a cigarette. In the glow of the firelight, the features looked almost animalistic, and Emily flinched slightly. Edward automatically moved in front of her to protect her. His voice was polite when he greeted the stranger. "Yes, it is a nice night out. Do you work here?"

They heard a low chuckle. "Oh, it's just one of the places I like to hang my hat every now and then."

The man stepped slowly out of the tent's shadow and into the carnival's lights. He fit into the carnival quite well. His skin was weird: it was tan, but it almost looked reddish. Like smoldering embers. He had long, greasy brown hair that hung down around his face. He was of average height but so thin, almost as if he were being eaten alive inside. In the carnival's flashing lights, it looked like a skeleton was standing there. A grinning skeleton with perfect white teeth—they looked slightly pointed.

The man's eyes were some sort of greenish-yellow mixture. The emotion in them looked wild and feverish, maybe even a little afraid. He had dark purple bruises under his eyes, like he hadn't slept in months. He was dressed like he worked in the carnival, in baggy blue pants and a red vest. He also wore a black top hat. Edward didn't like the looks of him at all.

"Oh, do you travel a lot?"

"You might say that." The man smiled as he moved closer and took a long drag from his cigarette.

"Ed?" Emily asked quietly from behind him.

"It's okay, Emily. He works here," Edward said reassuringly, but he didn't turn his back on the man.

The man's greenish-yellow eyes darted to Emily peeking out from behind Edward's back. He straightened. "Oh, excuse me, young lady. Where are my manners?" He swept off his top hat and gave a bow. "Invidia Green at your service. My tent's not far from here. I saw the two of you and thought to chat."

Emily nodded, but she didn't look any more at ease. Invidia straightened, placed his hat back on his head, and flicked the ash from his cigarette. He never stopped smiling.

"You said you have a tent not far from here. I don't remember seeing you. What kind of vendor are you?" Edward asked.

A card deck suddenly appeared in Invidia's hand. Edward had no idea where the deck had come from. He must have looked startled, because Invidia's grin widened as he went on to say, "I'm a card man myself. Beat me at cards and you win a prize."

"Cards, huh? What game do you play?"

"Any betting card games."

"Betting?"

"Yes," Invidia answered, then seemed to study him. "You a card man?"

"Not really," Edward answered sternly. He could feel Emily tugging on his arm and he said, "Well, it was nice meeting you. But we better be going."

"Ah, that's too bad. It's an easy win."

"No thanks," Edward answered as he started to turn away.

"It would only take a minute. Are you sure you don't want to play just one game?"

"Ed?" Emily said quietly.

"No. I don't think so. Have a good night," Edward said to Invidia, pushing Emily ahead of him.

"What about for five hundred dollars?"

Edward stopped. He turned back to the strange man. "Five hundred dollars? That's how much money you'd bet?"

Invidia grinned and tilted his head. "It's a lot of money, right? You win. You get an easy five hundred dollars. That kind of money isn't anything to sneeze on. It could help out with a lot of things. Help you get started with your life." His eyes moved deliberately to Emily again. "Maybe help a young couple get started with their lives. Am I right, man?"

"Edward. Let's go," Emily said from behind him, unable to pull him away.

Invidia looked at Emily and said, "It's nothing to be afraid of, young lady. Nothing wrong with a little game and wager."

"He's not interested," Emily said firmly.

"Well, he's not saying that, now is he?" Invidia looked back at Edward. Edward's face was emotionless. Invidia continued, "Life's hard, right? Big wad of cash in your pocket would help solve a lot of life's problems. Easy win. No joke."

Edward finally spoke. "Easy win, huh?"

"Edward," Emily said in surprise.

Invidia's grin was so wide that it showed all of his pointed teeth. He motioned behind him and said, "My tent's this way. Wouldn't take any time at all. And you could walk away a winner." And he strolled off, not pausing to see if they followed.

Edward stood there for a moment, and then he started after the man. Emily walked nervously beside him.

"Edward, don't. I don't trust him. Let's just go home, okay? We shouldn't be doing this."

"It's okay, Emily. Trust me," Edward answered and kept walking. He had money saved up from his job, but he always helped his mother pay the bills. The truth was he wasn't in any shape yet to move out without help from his mother, and he didn't want to do that to her. With five hundred dollars, not only would he be able to get started with his new life, but … He felt the wedding ring heavy in his pocket. He would be able to pay for a decent wedding for Emily. Edward pictured them living together in their new house as man and wife. He wanted that money.

"I do trust you. You know that. It's that Invidia freak I don't trust. Even if he did have that kind of money, he'd probably cheat or something. We'd never win."

"Just let me see what this is about, okay? It'll be fine." Edward finally looked down at Emily. Her pretty face was full of concern as she stared up at him. "Nothing will happen. And even if something does, I'll keep you safe. You know I will."

Emily took a deep breath and sighed. "I know. Just be careful, all right?"

"I will," Edward promised. Emily's worry was almost enough to make him stop walking. But the money. He wanted that damn money.

They came up to a tent. It was apart from the others and dimly lit. On top were flashing red letters that spelled CARD MAN.

"Step right up, my good young people. Don't be shy. Everyone is a winner tonight. Beat the card man and walk away a richer man. Five hundred dollars in cold cash. No lie," Invidia announced grandly from the tent's entrance.

They walked inside. Emily clutched Edward's hand. Invidia sat at a small wooden table. There was another chair pulled up opposite him. The card deck sat on the table. Invidia smiled up at them and motioned for Edward to take a seat. Edward sat down, Emily right behind his shoulder. Without a word Invidia pulled out a huge wad of cash and placed it on the table too.

"What game?" Edward asked seriously, staring at the money.

"How about twenty-one? You know that game?" Invidia asked.

Edward nodded and smiled. It was a game he had played a lot when he was younger. His father taught him how to play. Once all three of them had played on New Year's Eve. His father was in a good mood. It was one of Edward's very few memories of his dad that was actually good. Later he had played once in a while with his classmates.

"Five hundred dollars if you win," Invidia repeated.

"And if you win?" Edward asked.

Invidia grinned. "You have to give me something of yours."

"I don't have that much money."

"I don't want money."

"Then what?" Edward asked, confused.

"I'll let you know."

"Edward," Emily said nervously from behind him.

Edward was looking at Invidia. Invidia was smiling at him. "Have we got a deal?"

Edward glanced at the money. Sighing, he answered, "Yes."

"Then let's play." Invidia let Edward shuffle the deck. They were just normal playing cards, and Edward didn't see how Invidia could cheat him. Invidia took the cards back and dealt.

After a few rounds, Edward was confident he would win. His five cards added up to twenty. He recounted and was satisfied. He couldn't ask for another card. He had almost no chance of drawing a one, but unless Invidia's cards added up to twenty-one, Edward had won that game.

Emily had placed her hand on Edward's shoulder. He glanced up at her, and Emily gave a quick smile. She believed he had won the game too. She was still nervous, but they both could see the money sitting in front of them. As Invidia had said, it was no lie.

Invidia had three cards. When he offered Edward another card, Edward shook his head. Invidia smiled and asked, "Good hand, huh?"

"Wait and see," was Edward's only comment.

Invidia laughed and dealt himself another card. "Well, I do believe we have finally come to a standstill, my good sir. Ready to show me your hand?"

"Yeah. Twenty total," Edward said confidently and laid down his cards. He grinned up at Emily and she nodded, her smile confident as well as hopeful.

Invidia shook his head as though disappointed and said, "Good hand, Edward. Hardly can get better that ... but."

And Emily and Edward's smiles disappeared as Invidia slowly started laying his cards down. With each card laid down, the tension in the tent built. Edward felt a growing uneasiness. He'd made a bet. If he won, he would get five hundred dollars. But if he lost? What would he lose? Damn it, he should have made sure.

The wind suddenly picked up outside. The gust came out of nowhere and with such force that it blew the tent flaps straight back. And it was cold. It had been such a nice night, but suddenly it was freezing. Edward could see the goose bumps on his arms and feel the hair rise on the back of his neck. He had made an awful mistake in betting against this man.

Emily sensed it too. Her dark blue eyes widened in alarm and her ash-blond hair blew widely in the sudden wind. "Edward," she said fearfully.

Invidia had laid all of his cards down except for one. The cards on the table added up to twenty. The last card spun and danced in his fingers. Invidia had changed too. His greenish-yellow eyes were lit up feverishly, and something had happened to his skin. It had always been some sort of dull, reddish color, but now his skin looked like it was glowing, burning, a fire right below the surface. It looked like it hurt.

Invidia was watching them as he spun the card in his fingers, and suddenly he grinned. A huge grin stretched his cheeks and revealed all of his crystal-white fangs. The grin belonged to some madman, to something completely insane—or purely evil.

The card stopped at the top of his fingertips, and he turned it to them so they could see. The ace of spades was in his hand.

"You lose," Invidia said, grinning. And then he laughed. It was a laugh that would haunt Edward for the rest of his life, for it was the laugh of something not of this world.

"Edward!" Emily screamed.

"Emily!" Edward yelled, getting up so fast that the chair went flying backward. Edward reached out for Emily, knowing he had to get her out of here. He had to protect her. But a sudden flash of light struck, like lightning. One second Emily was standing there, ghost pale and wide-eyed, her eyes locked on him. The next she was gone. Edward's hand that had been only inches from her face was suddenly touching thin air.

"Emily!" Edward roared frantically, looking for her. She was nowhere to be seen.

The wind had picked up to a howl and it smacked him in the face. And it was so cold. Edward turned back to Invidia, not sure what he would face but determined to beat him if that's what it took to bring Emily back. Invidia was still laughing that manic, horrible laugh. Edward could hear him over the wind.

"Bastard! Where is she?" Edward bellowed. He drew back his fist to punch Invidia. But another flash of light came, and it struck him. It felt like pure energy moving through his whole body, and Edward couldn't move.

Suddenly a blackness overtook him. He heard the sound of the wind echoing in his head—or maybe it was Invidia's laughter. And then Edward heard no more.

Emily

She stood very still. Her head was bowed and her hair fell around her face. She would have brushed it back, but she couldn't seem to move. Emily didn't want to move; she was so tired. She had no idea where the sleepiness had come from, but it felt like her body was too heavy for her. Like she could collapse on the ground at any second.

Emily struggled to keep her thoughts clear, and her eyes opened. Something was wrong. She was outside: she knew that because there was grass beneath her feet. It was the air. The air felt heavy, almost like a huge downpour was going to happen at any second. It was so heavy that she had a hard time breathing, but that was okay because her lungs didn't seem to care if she breathed or not. It was dark here, and it was cold.

Emily had no idea where she was. Even that couldn't interest her enough to lift her head and look around. She just wanted to sleep. But there was a nagging thought at the back of her mind that wouldn't go away. What was it?

That was when it hit her that she was here alone. That couldn't be right, Edward should be with her. Edward was always with her. But her hand wasn't holding his, and that was enough to cause concern.

"Ed?" Emily asked, her voice sounding strange to her ears. It was so quiet here. No sounds at all. "Edward," Emily said again, her open hand closing and then opening again, as if searching for his. Edward would never have left her here. Where was Edward?

She tried to remember what they had been doing, but all she remembered seeing was Edward and then the flash of light. She also remember the sense of danger, of absolute dread and some of it came back, like her mind and body were at least trying now to be concerned for her well-being.

Where was Edward? They shouldn't be apart.

"Edward, I'm scared," Emily whispered.

"There is no reason to be afraid, Emily Thorn. I'm here," a voice suddenly said, the sound coming from every direction around her. It wasn't Edward's voice.

Two black riding boots appeared in Emily's small frame of vision, since all she had been looking at was the ground. Someone was standing right in front of her. Emily finally got the strength to look up, her head slowly tilting back. It took a lot of energy.

The man standing in front of her was someone she had never seen before. He wore a long black robe and held some kind of knife like weapon in his hand. It was a scary and massive weapon, and she knew it could easily rip her in half. The man was tall and strongly built. The hood of his robe covered his eyes. He was frowning. What she could see of his skin was almost transparent.

"Who are you?" Emily asked, her voice uninterested as her eyelids drooped.

"The Grim Reaper," he answered and took his hood down with one hand. He had a beautiful face although it was almost severe. He had short black hair and coal-colored eyes, the color of night itself.

"Am I dead?" Emily asked with no alarm.

"Not quite."

"Edward?"

"He's not here."

Emily allowed a ghost of a smile on her lips and said quietly, "That's good." When the Grim Reaper didn't ask, but raised his eyebrows in question, she went on to say slowly, "I don't want Edward to be here. I want him to be safe."

"You are safe. I won't let anything happen to you," the Grim Reaper answered. Emily nodded, unconcerned for her own safety.

They were silent for a moment and then he asked, "Why?"

"What?" Emily asked, lowering her head again.

"Why did you make the bet with Invidia? He is not a man of this world. He is not even a man."

Emily slowly raised her head again. She answered, "We didn't know. We were tricked."

The Grim Reaper nodded. His severe face softened just a little, and Emily thought she saw sympathy in his eyes. And sorrow. They were quiet again. The two of them seemed to stand there forever. Emily had no concept of time. But finally she asked, "Where are we?"

"In the land of the dead. This is where the souls travel to where they need to go."

Emily was not really surprised. This place seemed to match the Reaper's words. "What's going to happen to me now?" she asked.

"You cannot travel with the souls on the dead men's path. You aren't dead, but neither are you alive."

"Then what will happen to me?"

"You will sleep."

"Sleep?"

"Yes. In the garden."

"For how long?" Emily asked, having trouble following the conversation. Her neck barely supported the weight of her head.

"Until the end of time," the Grim Reaper answered without emotion. "Come."

Emily had no idea how she would be able to follow his command. But although she knew he wouldn't harm her, she also knew that his words were not something someone could ignore. The Grim Reaper started to walk away, and to Emily's surprise, her feet followed him like they had a mind of their own.

They were in the woods somewhere, and it was night there. She had no concept of distance or how long they had walked. Suddenly she realized they were walking through a huge iron gate and into a garden. The name of the garden was engraved in the iron at the top of the gate: Forget-Me-Not Garden. They continued to walk, and Emily saw that there were forget-me-not flowers everywhere in several shades of blue, white, and light purple. The garden was so big that Emily couldn't see the end to it.

A fog came up heavily and rose to Emily's knees. There were stones too; some of them had people sleeping on them. They didn't move when Emily and the Grim Reaper walked by. It was almost like a cemetery.

"Why are you crying?" The Grim Reaper asked without turning around to look at her.

Emily hadn't realized she was until he spoke. Then she noticed the tears falling from her cheeks. One landed on her pale white hand.

The Grim Reaper stopped at a stone slab. It was long and stuck out from the fog. Forget-me-not flowers grew around it.

"I'm just sad," Emily whispered, coming to a stop too.

"You will sleep peacefully. You will have no sense of time or place here. Only sleep until I come to wake you at the end," the Grim Reaper said in a voice that was not kind or unkind. Emily realized he was trying to offer her some comfort.

"That's not why I'm sad," Emily said as another tear fell. When the Reaper raised his eyebrows again in question, Emily explained, "It's my boyfriend, Edward. He'll look for me and won't be able to find me. I should be with him."

When he didn't answer, Emily smiled softly again. "Maybe I'll dream about him."

After a while, the Grim Reaper finally said, "This garden is known as Forget-Me-Not Garden. It was created for only one purpose: to be a safe haven of rest for those who have nowhere else to go. It's for those who are not alive but not dead either. Somewhere in-between. The flowers represent memory, so that the ones who rest here can be remembered by those who loved them and won't fade away. Also, if someone from the world of the living ever wanted to bring one who was sleeping here back, he or she might be able to do so. But only if that person had a strong will and a stronger spirit. Not many who are living have ever made it here to retrieve those who are sleeping."

Emily's eyes widened for a moment and she smiled. The Grim Reaper repeated again, "Few have ever made it here, Emily. And even if they do come … they can't just enter. A price must be paid."

"Edward will come for me," Emily answered, sure in her answer.

The Grim Reaper didn't reply, but motioned for her to lie down on the stone slab. Although Emily felt dead on her feet, she didn't want to go to sleep. To stall for a moment, Emily asked quietly, "Everyone here is sleeping so peacefully. Will I sleep like that?"

"Yes."

Emily nodded and then realized that the only reason she could stall for time was because he was allowing her to. But his orders had been given, and she found herself walking to her stone slab. He helped her up on it, because Emily was so tired. She lay down and inhaled the sweet fragrance of the forget-me-not flowers. She had no fear as she looked up at the Grim Reaper standing respectfully at her side and looking down at her.

"May I ask you something?" Emily asked, focusing on him, trying to stay awake.

"Yes."

"Why are you the Grim Reaper? You almost seem normal. So why you?"

A very faint smile touched his lips at the *almost normal* part. Emily didn't think he smiled often. But the smile left as quickly as it came when he answered, "Someone has to be the Grim Reaper. As life enters into the world, death must leave it. That is the balance of this world, and there must be someone to maintain the balance … always."

Although Emily was fascinated by his explanation, she realized that he hadn't quite answered her question. Or maybe he had and she'd missed it. She was too tired to figure it out now.

"Edward will come," Emily repeated as she closed her eyes. "He knows forget-me-nots are my favorite flowers. He'll find a way to me."

The Grim Reaper only nodded once to let her know he had heard her and answered solemnly, "Good night, Emily."

Emily didn't answer. Her one last thought before she fell into a deep sleep was about being held in Edward's arms as they watched the sunset on the hill. At the carnival, Edward had promised her, "Nothing will happen. And even if something does, I'll keep you safe. You know I will."

Edward. She loved Edward with all of her heart. She hoped that no matter if they were apart or she couldn't ever be with him again, he knew that was the truth. She let herself be swept away by the abysses.

CHAPTER FOUR

Fate

Edward

*H*e didn't know if he was dreaming or not. He was unconscious, but what he was seeing wasn't dreams. They were memories, like flashbacks. And they were all about Emily. They were going by so fast that they were blending together. He heard her voice: *"Edward, isn't the sunset pretty?"* All of their sunsets flashed in his memories. There were a lot of them, and the one on the Ferris wheel was the last.

"*I need you, Edward,*" came her voice again, and he remembered her taking his hand after kissing him in front of her dad's house.

Then there were all the memories of Emily's smiling face and the look she wore when she looked up at him. *"I love you, Edward Mikes. Don't ever forget that."*

Edward became nervous. All of these flashing memories of Emily were beautiful, but where was Emily? He tried to wake up then. All he knew was he needed to find her. But one last memory came into his mind. He didn't see Emily's face. He just heard her question echoing in his head: *"Do you know what my favorite flower is, Ed?"*

Edward jerked awake, his eyes flying open. He was lying on his back in the grass. Stars were shining up in the sky. But hadn't there been lightning just a second ago?

Emily. Edward sat up, looking around. There was no one besides him there. He was on the outskirts of the carnival, away from the rest of the tents.

"Emily," Edward called, standing up. She was nowhere to be seen.

That was when he remembered Invidia. He remembered the money, the game of twenty-one. He had lost the bet. Edward remembered Invidia's wide grin and he remembered that laugh. Then Emily was calling to him. The flash of lightning, and Emily disappeared. He turned on Invidia—and then nothing.

Edward suddenly realized that not only were Emily and Invidia missing, but so was Invidia's tent. It had all just vanished. He stared at the spot where the tent with the flashing lights should have been. There was no way he had been unconscious long enough for Invidia to take the tent down, was there?

Edward's back straightened. His hands clenched into fists, and his eyes hardened. None of that mattered. Emily was gone. Invidia had taken her from him; Edward was sure of that. And he was going to get her back. He was going to find Emily and kill Invidia with his bare hands for taking her.

Edward started thinking in a cold, focused manner that he had learned back when his father was alive and in one of his moods. More than once, it had saved Edward and his mother from being beaten.

Invidia might have taken Emily, and God knew where his freaking tent had gone, but Edward figured that they couldn't have gotten far. He knew Emily never would have gone with Invidia without fighting like hell. He should be able to reach them, wherever they were. He started to move, but suddenly he heard a soft sigh. "You made a bet, didn't you?"

He whirled around, startled that he was no longer alone. The voice was somehow familiar to him. It was soft and feminine, but he knew that was not why he had heard it before. "Who's there?" he called.

A young woman stepped toward him, like she had just appeared out of thin air. Edward recognized her as the woman he had seen earlier that day in the main tent—the woman he'd bumped into. He remembered that she had seemed alarmed when she looked at him. She was just as beautiful now, but Edward was immediately suspicious of her. She might know something of this situation. Hell, she might even be with that freak Invidia.

The woman wasn't smiling as she walked up to him. She looked almost sad, and also irritated. "You made a deal with someone you never should have messed with. You bet against a demon and lost. And now she is gone. The Demon Envy sent her soul away."

"Demon?" Edward asked, shocked. "He wasn't a demon. He said his name was Invidia Green. He said he was a card man."

A very slight smile touched her lips. "Green? That's funny. Envy has many names he's developed over the thousands of years he has been on this earth. Invidia is an ancient name. It's a Latin word that means envy. And I'm sure you understand green, right? Green with envy. He must have been in a joking mood."

"That can't be …" Then Edward remembered Invidia's grin, and he heard the laughter again. The laughter had been demonic, the sound of sheer madness and evil. It sent chills down his spine. He remembered the lightning and the freezing wind and how Invidia's skin almost looked like it was burning from the inside out. Invidia had not belonged to this world. He was demon, and Edward had bet against him.

As if reading his mind, the young woman repeated solemnly, "You never should have bet against him."

"Where is he?" Edward asked, weary but resigned.

She looked surprised when she answered, "He's gone. Why do you want to know?"

"He took my girlfriend. I have to find them."

"After everything you saw? After seeing his power and knowing his true identity, you'd still go after him?"

"He has Emily. I'd follow him into hell if I had to. Anything to save Emily."

She look amused as well as a little impressed when she answered, "He's not in hell. He won't be until his job is done on this earth. But he's not here. He has disappeared somewhere we can't follow. It doesn't matter; he doesn't have your girlfriend."

"Then where is she?" Edward asked.

A hard look came across her lovely face. She asked again, "Why do you care? You made a bet with the Demon Envy and lost her in the process. But you are still in one piece. Why bother with her now?"

Edward's jaw tightened and his hands clenched. He wasn't angry at what the woman had said so much. He was angry because he knew she was right. Emily was gone, and it was all his fault. And not having Emily with him now? It hurt like hell. Like a part of him had been taken, part of his soul.

"Look, lady. I didn't know. I didn't know that I was betting against a freaking demon. I didn't know that if I lost, I'd lose my girlfriend. And you can be damn sure that if I'd known any of this, I sure as hell wouldn't have made that bet to begin with! This is all just crazy! Where is she? Where is Emily? I need to find her." Edward ran his hand through his hair.

The woman didn't respond for a moment. She just stood there staring at him, surprise in her eyes. Edward stood there too, wanting to apologize for blowing up at her, wanting her help, and restless because he wanted to start looking for Emily.

Finally she answered, "May I ask you something? How far are you willing to go to find Emily?"

Without hesitation, Edward replied, "Whatever it takes. I will do whatever I have to bring her back."

"Why?"

"What do you mean, why? I love her. She's mine and I have to protect her. Every second we stand here talking, Emily's going to be wondering why I'm not with her,"

Edward said, his hand clenched so tightly his knuckles turned white.

"Emily's not here anymore. She's not alive anymore," the woman said. She watched Edward's face for a moment, then continued, "She's not quite dead yet either. Envy didn't kill her. He sent her body and soul to the land of the dead. It's a place in-between, where all souls go to journey to where they need to be. But Emily's not dead, and so her soul can't travel with the others."

Edward wanted to tell her to stop talking crazy. Yet Emily was gone with a flash of lightning, and Invidia Green was undoubtedly a demon, so he guessed he really couldn't afford not to believe her. Instead he asked very calmly, "What will happen to her?"

"She's been taken to the garden."

"Garden?"

"The Forget-Me-Not Garden, a place that exists for those like Emily. It's for souls that have nowhere to go, that can't travel with the others. It's the place her soul will sleep forever."

"No!" Edward yelled, a cold panic gripping his heart. "I won't let that happen to her. Where is this garden? How do I get to her? Please show me."

The woman bit her bottom lip. She lowered her gaze to the ground. "There is a way. But … it won't be easy for you."

"I don't care. Please show me."

"Your Emily will be safe at the garden. No one will ever be able to hurt her, and she will sleep peacefully there until the end of time."

Edward imagined Emily sleeping in a strange garden in a place of death, her skin cold and pale, her body still and lifeless. He imagined his life without ever seeing her again. That was completely unacceptable.

"Emily doesn't belong in some garden. She belongs with me. I will find her and bring her home, with or without your help. But if you would help me, I'd really appreciate it."

The woman finally looked him full in the face again. She asked him, "Your mind is made up, then?"

"Yes."

She studied him for a moment. "Fine. I will help you. Follow me."

She turned and started walking. Edward quickly went after her. The carnival was almost completely dark now, and Edward figured that everyone must be gone. Everyone except for the ones who worked there.

"Thank you. My name is Edward."

"Don't thank me yet, Edward. I'm Fate."

Fate. He suddenly remembered Joshua and Rose talking about her earlier that day. Fate was some kind of fortune-teller. Obviously she was something more.

"Earlier today, I'm pretty sure I saw you at the main tent after the acts. I bumped into you."

"Yes."

"You looked like you wanted to say something to me."

"I did. Edward, you have a hint of fate about you. I've been sensing a change lately. I knew something or someone was coming. When I saw you, I knew you were it."

"What do you mean by change?"

"I'll explain later. This is my trailer. Come in," Fate said as they came up to a small trailer. A tent was set up in front of it.

Edward followed her in. They were in some kind of living area. It was dimly lit by candles. There was a table, but nothing was on it. Edward kind of expected to see cards or a crystal ball.

As if reading his mind, Fate stated, "All of my props are in my tent."

"Props? So you don't tell the future?"

"Everyone has to make a living. Can I see into the future? No. That being said, I'm not your usual type of woman either."

"I can tell," Edward said. His gaze fell on a big barn owl sitting on a peg, gazing back at him. Its huge yellow eyes stared into his.

"That's Ramona," Fate murmured glancing at the owl. "I'm sure she's ready to go hunting for the night." The owl sat another moment staring at the two of them before hooting and flying out the opened door.

"Nice pet."

"Ramona's not really a pet. It's her choice to come home every day, and she always does. I found her when she was a chick. The poor thing must have fallen from her nest. I took care of her. She's been with me ever since, but she always has the option to leave if she wants to," Fate answered as she rummaged through her things.

"What are you looking for?" Edward asked.

"For something we might need. Everything else will have to wait until we're on the path."

"Path?"

"Dead Man's Path. It's the main path that all souls will travel on their journeys to where they will rest for all eternity."

"Oh," Edward said dryly.

Fate chuckled softly. "The path will only open to us at midnight tonight, the night of All Hallows' Eve. Once we make it on the path, we have only until dawn. By then we must come back to the world of the living, or we will be trapped there forever."

Edward ran a hand through his hair and said, "This is so crazy. How do you know all this?"

Fate was silent a moment before she answered, "Let's just say I have some experience in this."

Edward sighed. His gaze fell on a picture on the wall. It was a picture of Fate, and she was with a guy. They were outside. Both were smiling. His arm was around her shoulders.

"Who's that in the picture with you?"

Without looking at the picture, Fate said quietly, "That's Zachary. Zach."

The picture looked kind of old, like it had been taken a while ago. Edward was tempted to see if the year was on the back of it, but that would have been rude. And Fate was so young looking, he didn't think she was more than a couple years older than him.

"Is he your husband?"

"He was my boyfriend. We were engaged, but something happened."

"I'm sorry."

"It's okay. He'll always be my soul mate and my one true love. Things like that come only once in a lifetime."

Edward wanted to ask more, but she exclaimed, "Ah! Here it is." And she held up a basket. He didn't look to see what was in it. For all he knew, the contents were eyeballs. He really didn't want to take anything more at this point.

Fate turned to smile at him. She said, "We have what we need. But before we continue, please sit down. We have a moment, and there is something that I have to explain to you."

Edward nodded and sat down at the table. Fate took a seat across from him. Edward had a wild thought that she was going to pull out a crystal ball and start telling him his future. But this was something real and much more important.

Seeing Fate face-on in the light of her home, Edward was struck again by how lovely she was. She seemed so young, but her emerald-green eyes held a wisdom that was far past her years. Her eyes also held sorrow, the kind that never heals, that settles into one's very soul and becomes a part of it. Edward wondered if the man called Zachary had anything to do with it.

"How old are you?" Edward asked suddenly. To his surprise, Fate burst out laughing. It was a chime-like laugh, pretty. Edward missed Emily's laugh. The hole in his chest ached with a new intensity.

"A lady never reveals her true age, Edward," Fate said, still chuckling.

"Right. Sorry. It was a rude question."

"No. It's fine. I'm still not going to answer. But why ask at all, given the circumstances?"

"It's just … you look too young to know so much. Wise for your age, I guess."

Fate's smile turned sad and the sorrow returned to her eyes. Edward was sorry to see it.

"I guess I am," Fate murmured. "Let's get back to business, shall we?"

Edward nodded. He pressed his lips in a grim line as he leaned forward to listen.

"As I've already explained, Emily will sleep in Forget-Me-Not Garden. But the flowers that grow in the garden represent memory. If someone from the living has the strength of will and of heart, he may be able to travel to the land of the dead and retrieve the one he lost. But only on All Hallows' Eve, and only until dawn. Do you understand, Edward? If you can't bring Emily back before that time, both of you will be forever lost in the land of the dead."

"I understand," Edward said without fear. "I would rather be lost with her forever in some garden than live life without her. I won't return without her."

Fate looked touched. "Emily is lucky to have you in her life."

Edward frowned and looked down at his hands folded on the table. "Not really. It's my fault she's there in the first place."

"Envy is very cunning. What hope did you have against a demon that is thousands of years old?"

"But why us? Why did he come after us? Why take Emily away from me?" Edward asked, his hands clenching into fists. To his surprise, Fate's paler and much smaller hand was suddenly there, on top of his. He looked back up at her. Fate looked very sad and vulnerable.

"All Envy is, all he will ever be, is jealousy. That is the only emotion he is allowed to feel—jealousy of everyone for things he can never have. Like hope, or faith, or love. These are powerful emotions. He saw the love between you and Emily. That love would have driven him insane with jealousy because he can almost feel it, but never truly know it for himself. That's why he came after you two. What he can't have, he will seek to destroy."

"If Emily and I are able to return here, will he come after us again?" Edward asked, wondering how one could kill a demon. He would fight like hell before letting Envy separate him and Emily again.

Fate smiled faintly and answered, "You would never win. What drives Envy and the rest of his siblings is an evil far beyond our imagining. Best to leave him to someone who could beat him. Anyway, Envy won't ever come into your life again. Trust me."

Edward didn't know how Fate could possibly know all of these things, but he did know that he trusted her. He had to.

Fate leaned back in her chair and a grave expression showed on her face. "Envy is no longer the problem. There is one more thing you need to know before entering into the land of the dead."

"Great." Edward sighed and straightened in his chair, ready to hear.

"In the land of the dead there must be order. Think of the souls traveling to their destinations and how chaotic it would be if no one took charge over them. If no one guarded Dead Man's Path."

Edward nodded in understanding and Fate continued, "The one who guards the path and the souls is the same one who put those souls there."

Edward raised his eyebrows in question.

"The Grim Reaper, Edward."

An image of a shadowy figure holding a scythe and having a skull for a head flashed in his mind. "The Grim Reaper? He's real?"

"Yes. The Reaper's sole duty is to maintain the balance between life and death. As life enters into the world, death must leave it. The Grim Reaper walks the path of nightfall and death. He guides the souls to where they need to go. And he is the one who is guarding the gates of the Forget-Me-Not Garden."

The thought of the Grim Reaper around Emily sent chills down Edward's spine and panic into his mind. He had to protect her. "How can I save Emily?" he asked, starting to stand up.

"Calm down. The Grim Reaper would never harm her. He may represent death, but his concern is to maintain order. The Reaper would have been the one to guide Emily to the garden, where she will be safe."

"So he's a good guy?"

"Bad or good, who knows? He simply is."

"How do I get past him?"

"It is impossible to get past him, Edward. We will be in his world. The moment we enter, he will know of it."

"Then how do I get to Emily?" Edward asked frustrated.

"There is a price that must be paid to enter the gates. A very costly price. But if you pay it, Emily will be able to return to the land of the living."

"Then I'll pay the price," Edward replied without hesitation.

Fate allowed another faint smile. "Just like that, huh?"

Edward nodded. "Just like that."

"You're a very serious young man. In a way you remind me of my Zachary. He was serious too."

Edward allowed himself to smile. "I get that a lot. My mom always called me her responsible man."

"I can see why." A new sadness and concern spread over Fate's face. "Your mother will be worried about you, Edward."

"And Emily's dad will be worried about her. I have to get her back, Fate. I have to," Edward said, the smile gone and forgotten.

Fate whispered, "I understand."

From outside they could hear Ramona's hooting.

Fate straightened and stood up. "Time's almost come. Three minutes till midnight. Let's go." Fate glanced at the clock on the wall and turned to leave the trailer. Edward followed her again.

They stepped out in the cool night air. Edward expected her to start walking, but instead she stopped. She took something out of her basket. Edward saw that it was a bag of salt. She sprinkled it around them until there was a big circle surrounding them and a trail of salt pointing to the woods. The wind picked up, and Edward was reminded with a chill of the sudden gust of wind when he made the bet with Invidia. One thing he was sure of was that something was going to happen.

Fate suddenly spoke in a soft voice that became louder as she continued. "Mind of my mind, body of my body, soul of my soul, I bid the door to open. Let the living join the dead and walk on the same path, so we may find what we have lost. And when dawn draws near, let us part and return from whence we came. Open the door!"

Lightning suddenly flashed and the wind picked up to a howl. The air was so cold it sent shivers up Edward's spine. Fate's raven-black hair swirled around her head and her black cape rose around her body like the wings of that very raven. Her skin was so pale it looked almost transparent in the brightness of the flashing lightning.

"Edward," Fate said softly, although he could still hear her over the howl of the wind somehow. "In just a moment the portal to the land of the dead will open and there will be no going back. Are you sure this is what you want?"

"Yes," Edward replied without hesitation. "I have to find Emily."

Fate nodded and turned to face forward. "The time has come."

Edward braced himself and looked ahead of Fate. He saw a light appear in front of her. The light got bigger and bigger until it was as tall as Edward.

"Follow me," Fate said and stepped forward. She kept walking until she was at the light. One more step, and to Edward's surprise she disappeared. She just vanished into thin air.

Edward thought that his mom must be wondering where he was right now. And David would probably be thinking about killing him. The last conversation they had suddenly came back to him.

"You take good care of my daughter. Hear me?"

"Yes, sir. I'll keep her safe and bring her back home to you."

"Holding you to that."

"Don't worry. I'm a man of my word."

"I know you are, son."

Emily's dad had called him son. Old Dave saying that to him meant more to Edward than he would have ever guessed. A grim determination settled over Edward as he stared into the portal. He hardly noticed the wind or lightning now. Emily was there somewhere on the other side, waiting for him.

"I'll bring her back. I'll find Emily and bring her home. I will protect Emily. I swear it on my soul," Edward promised in a hard, determined voice with Ramona the owl as his witness. He stepped through the portal.

CHAPTER FIVE

Dead Man's Path

Fate

The first few years without Zachary hadn't been pretty. Each day without him passed so agonizing slowly, and Fate couldn't cope. She felt that life was meaningless. Food lost taste. Smiles were forced. She grew paler and thinner, and she was always cold, like a permanent winter had settled into her bones.

Fate dreamed about Zachary every night. She would see his face. Feel his skin that was warm again, that had blood running underneath. Hear his breathing. She would dream that she was lying in his arms, finally at peace. And then she would wake up and the loneliness would be unbearable. The sense of loss was always with her. Fate struggled through life, no longer feeling like she had a purpose.

For one night a year, on All Hallows' Eve, Zach was actually there with her, and she could really touch him. She was so happy. Zachary was never the same after that one fateful night. In life he had always been the serious type, but in death he was just a part of his former self. So quiet, so still, so beautiful. But it didn't matter, because he was still Zach. Her Zach.

The very first night he came back to her, Fate had been home alone, sitting at the kitchen table. Her parents had gone out for the night. It had taken all of Fate's acting skills to convince her parents that she was all right and could be left alone.

She couldn't blame them for being hesitant. For several months after Zachary disappeared, Fate had been sunk in a deep depression, unable to even attempt to care about anything. Nights were the worst. Fate didn't know how many times her mother had run into her room after she woke up from a nightmare, screaming. And then she would cry. Fate cried more during those months than she ever had in her life. The only thing that got her through the first unbearably long year was the faint hope that Zachary would come.

So she waited alone, sitting at the table. She hadn't been sure if he would truly come. Everything about that night seemed unreal and hazy. But one thing she remembered clearly: Zachary had promised her, had promised he would come to her. And he had never broken a promise to her, not once.

The sun went down on All Hallows' Eve. Then she heard the quiet knock on the door.

When she got up to answer the door, her steps seemed slow to her, as if she were afraid to open the door. What if it wasn't Zachary? What would she do then?

She got to the door. It was completely silent on the other side, but she could feel a presence there. There was a chill leaking through the door. It wasn't of this world. The doorknob was ice-cold when she turned it.

"Please," Fate whispered, and a sob caught in her throat. She opened the door all the way.

Zachary was standing there, so pale that his skin was transparent. Cold radiated off of him and he was still. There was no life in him. But he was looking down at her with the same coal-colored eyes, and she knew that it was him and that everything that had happened a year ago was real. She wasn't crazy after all.

They stood there, looking at each other as if stuck in time. Fate didn't realize she was crying until she felt the tears sliding down her cheeks. Then she threw herself into his arms, openly weeping. His body was so cold that it seemed to suck the air out of her lungs, but she didn't care. She didn't dare let him go.

"Fate," she heard him murmur. Even his voice seemed still and lifeless. But she could still feel his love for her—like him, eternal. Like her too, she supposed.

"You came back," Fate sobbed against his chest as she buried her face in him. His scent was gone. He used to smell like leather and soap. Now breathing him in was like breathing in cold winter air.

"I promised I would," Zachary said.

"Then … it's all true? What happened that night was real?"

"Yes."

Fate took a shaky breath and hugged him more tightly. Her teeth were chattering. She wanted some of her body's warmth to seep into his, but she knew it never would. No amount of heat would warm him again.

"You're shivering, Fate," Zachary whispered. She could hear the worry in it, but she wouldn't let him go. Not tonight.

"This is real, right? I'm not dreaming? You're really here?" Fate asked on another sob.

Instead of answering she felt his arms wrap around her. She didn't know how long they stood like that, just holding each other.

"I missed you," Fate said against his chest.

"I missed you too," Zach whispered.

And Fate smiled. Without Zach it felt like a part of her heart had been taken, leaving a huge hole in her chest. With him here, it was like her heart became whole again. Like coming home.

But she suddenly felt weird. It was like her body was weightless and she was floating away. "Zach?" Fate asked.

She heard him sigh, and he pulled away from her. She panicked when she felt him leaving, and then she almost fell. But he caught her. The next thing she knew, they were in her bedroom, and he was setting her down on her bed. How they got up the stairs and through her door, she had no idea. Then again, Zach could do many things that were impossible.

She sat there, taking deep breaths and waiting to feel her feet on the ground. Zach stood over her, watching her with a frown, but it was for her health that he was concerned. Fate almost laughed. He always wore that same look whenever he was worried for her. So stern, like he would take down an army for her safety. He could now, without any trouble at all.

"Why am I so dizzy?" Fate asked faintly as she leaned back against the wall.

"I'm the Grim Reaper now. Hugging me is the same as hugging death. It's not healthy. You risk death when you embrace me."

"Okay," she answered without concern.

"Okay? Fate, I'm a danger to you now," Zach said sternly, emotion finally showing on his beautiful, stony face.

"No. I belong with you. Don't leave me, Zach," Fate said, panicking again.

"I'm right here," he said gently.

"Please, sit with me," Fate begged.

Zachary sighed but sat down next to her, being careful not to touch her. But Fate couldn't bear not touching him.

"Please hold my hand, Zach."

"Fate …"

"Please. I can't bear not being able to touch you," Fate whispered, tears starting to fall again. Zachary gently took her hand in his. His hand engulfing hers was every bit as cold as the rest of him. She didn't care and clung to his hand.

"Please don't cry anymore," Zachary said softly.

"You know, I've cried a lot since you left."

"Of course I know."

"You can hear me?" Fate asked, surprised.

"I'm always with you, Fate. Always."

Fate scooted closer to him until her thigh was touching his black robe and her shoulder was pressed against his. She laid her head on his shoulder and sighed, closing her eyes. It was just like old times. Zachary sighed too and laid his head on hers.

"You smell the same," Zachary murmured.

"Are you tired?"

"I'm never tired now. Sleep is beyond me."

"I'm sorry," Fate whispered.

"For what?"

"I did this to you. You must hate me."

"I could never hate you. What I am now is of my own free will. And I would have chosen this again and again if it meant saving you."

"Will you kiss me, Zachary?"

"I don't think it's safe."

"I don't care. Please?"

She lifted her head to look up at him, and he was looking back. His face was as still and expressionless as a statue, but in his eyes she saw what she thought looked like yearning. She didn't ask for permission, only closed her eyes and tilted her face to him. She couldn't hear him, but she could feel the coldness of him coming closer, wrapping around her like a blanket of snow.

"Fate." And then his lips were on hers. His lips were freezing, and it felt like her very life was being sucked out of her. But he kissed her the same way he had when he was alive. She desperately wrapped her arms around his neck and ran her hands through his hair. She felt his arms wrap around her. He kissed her more deeply, and she felt such a happiness. This was Zach, her Zach. He had come back to her.

In the end he pulled away first. Fate's face had gone numb, like all the blood had left her body, and she was shivering violently. She collapsed against him and waited for her heart to start beating normally again.

In the end they sat like that for most of the night, leaning against one another. At times they were silent, enjoying one another's presence. Then Fate would ask him questions about what it was like to be the Grim Reaper. He answered her questions truthfully. She listened to the low rumble of his voice, like thunder in the distance.

It started to rain around midnight, and they sat there listening to it.

"I'd almost forgotten the sound of rain on this side," Zach said thoughtfully.

"It's lonely without you."

"I have never left your side."

"I didn't know you were with me."

"Perhaps with time you will be able to tell."

The rain stopped. Fate could feel herself drifting in a sleeplike state, but she wouldn't let herself fall asleep. Not with Zachary finally here. She could have stayed like that forever, and it seemed like no time had passed before she heard Zach sigh. "It's almost dawn."

Fate sat up and said very simply, "Don't leave me."

"I have to go. I can feel the souls starting to become restless without someone to guide them."

And of course the only one who could guide them was the Grim Reaper.

Zachary stood. Fate tried to stand up too, but spending the night beside death itself had left her very unsteady on her feet. She would have fallen had Zach not caught her. He held her weight easily with one hand.

"You should eat more," he scolded gently.

"I will," Fate answered and wrapped her arms around his waist. She looked up into his face and asked, "Will you come back to me?"

"Always," he promised solemnly and without hesitation.

Fate could feel tears gathering but she firmly held them back for Zach's sake. Zachary kissed her softly on the head and pulled away from her. He started to turn away, but she had a question that she was afraid to ask.

"Zachary Conner, do you still love me?"

He stopped and turned back to her. Such a beautiful and emotionless face. Maybe that's why she had been afraid to ask him; she couldn't read his expressions anymore.

"You hold my heart, Fate. Now and forever. No matter what has changed about me, nothing could ever change the love I have for you."

Fate smiled, and this time she couldn't help the tears that started to fall. There wasn't any holding them back. She ignored them and answered, "I love you too, Zachary. So much."

The faintest of smiles touched his lips, and he turned away from her again. She thought he would leave her, and she lowered her head, trying to hold it together.

"Will you wait for me?"

She looked up quickly. His back was to her, and he was standing so still. But he was waiting for her answer. She smiled, even though she wasn't sure if he could see it. "Of course, silly. I'll wait for you forever."

He nodded and was gone. She fell on the bed, relishing the coldness she still felt from where Zachary had been sitting. It was the only proof that he had been there. She sat and watched the sun come up. She didn't let herself cry, because now she knew Zachary could see her. She had never hated dawn so much as now.

Edward

Edward heard someone say his name. He saw Emily's smiling face. Her long ash-blond hair falling around her face. Her laughing blue eyes staring up at him. He reached a hand out to her, and she was gone.

"Edward?"

"Emily?" Edward asked.

"No, Edward. It's me. We have to go now."

Edward opened his eyes and he saw Fate standing over him.

"Are you okay?" Fate asked, worried.

Edward sat up and rubbed his head, which felt as heavy as lead. "I'm okay." He looked at Fate, who appeared tired and weak. "Are you all right, Fate?"

Fate smiled and answered, "Yes. I'm fine."

"I'm glad." Edward smiled and stood too. His body felt like it weighed a ton.

Fate must have noticed his struggle because she said, "It's the air in this world. To us living, it makes our bodies feel heavy. We may also have more trouble breathing here. This world just isn't very compatible with the living."

"I see," Edward answered and looked around. They were in the woods. Fog covered the ground, and it was dark and cold. It was a calm place, but unnerving just the same. "So this is the land of the dead."

"Yes. We have arrived."

"All right." Edward straightened his back and rolled his shoulders to adjust to the new environment. "You said the Grim Reaper will know we are here?"

"Yes."

"Then let's get moving. If you're ready."

Fate smiled and answered, "I was going to ask you the same thing."

Edward grinned. "Please lead the way."

"Follow me. We don't have long."

Edward heard hooting. He looked up at one of the trees and saw Fate's owl, Ramona, staring down at them.

"I didn't know Ramona followed me into the portal," Edward said, thinking it was a weird thing for an owl to do.

"She didn't," Fate replied, glancing up at Ramona. "Owls have no limits between worlds. They come and go freely. To her, we are in her world."

"Really?" Edward stared up at Ramona's wise face.

"Yes." Fate looked at Edward with a smile. "Did you know the Native Americans believe that if you heard an owl hooting at night, it is calling your name and you will die soon?"

"A pleasant thought," Edward replied dryly, thinking about how many times he had heard Ramona hooting just tonight.

Fate laughed. "Let us continue. Ramona may follow us, so don't be surprised if you continue to hear her."

"Okay," Edward agreed, and they went on.

Fate carried her basket. Edward followed right behind her. She seemed to know where they were going, and as unsettling as that was for Edward, he was relieved to know they were unlikely to get lost.

On the other hand, Edward knew there were several things he would have to figure out. Pieces of the puzzle were missing. But not right now. Right now, Fate was the only one who could help him. He was thankful for her guidance and her presence.

Fate led him through the woods. Edward followed in silence. A thought rose in his mind. If he was going up against the Grim Reaper, he should understand more about him. "Has the Grim Reaper been around for as long as the Demon Envy?"

Fate was quiet for a moment, but finally answered without looking at him. "For as long as life and death have been in this world, there has been a Grim Reaper. But not the same one."

"What do you mean by that?"

"The Reaper now at one time was alive."

"So he was human once?" Edward asked.

"Yes."

"What happened to make him the Grim Reaper?"

"He paid the price."

"Price?"

"Yes, Edward. Someone has to be the Grim Reaper. If there was no reaping, or if there was no one to guide the dead, there would an imbalance between life and death. Chaos would enter the world of the living and of the dead. There must always be a Grim Reaper. Always. The present one paid the price. And that is why he is who he is."

"So he was punished or something?"

"Being the Grim Reaper is not a punishment."

"Why did he have to pay a price, then?"

Fate suddenly stopped and turned to him. She stared up in his eyes, her lovely, pale face sad and tired, and answered, "He saved someone. He wanted to protect that person he cared about. And so he did. The price was paid."

A chill went down Edward's spine, and he asked no more questions for the time. Fate walked on, seeming to drift through the woods like a ghost herself. Edward followed, realization slowly sinking in. Everything that Fate had said …

Edward's eyes widened. It felt like a lump of ice was lodged down his throat. One memory was clear as day in his head: "*There is a price that must be paid to enter the gates. A very costly price. But if you pay it, Emily will be able to return to the land of the living.*"

Emily's life depended on Edward's actions. The burden weighed down his shoulders, but he squared them, accepting the weight and the responsibility. A grim determination settled over him then like a cloak. There would be no going back after this. Edward marched forward, eyes open and prepared.

After a time, Fate stopped again and whispered, "We are about to join Dead Man's Path. Where the souls travel. It is important to remain calm. If you need to talk, make sure to whisper. Make no sudden movements. The souls are usually quiet and should remain unaware of us. But if something happens that causes them alarm, they will become restless. For now the Grim Reaper has let us travel in his world, but he would have to interfere if the souls became upset. Do you understand, Edward?"

"I understand," Edward whispered grimly.

"Also. If by any chance you see someone that you knew back when they were alive, you are to leave them be. Don't draw attention to yourself. They are souls that only wish to travel undisturbed. Understand?"

Edward swallowed but answered, "I understand."

"Good. Let's go." Fate continued to walk, and Edward followed. He felt breathless and, for the first time, scared.

For a moment he didn't notice anything. Suddenly they were on what seemed to be a wide path. The stepped onto it and started walking again.

Edward felt a presence. He turned and saw a man walking next to him. It was easy to tell that the man was dead, for Edward could see through him. Edward choked back a either a gasp or a curse—he wasn't sure which. The soul didn't look at him or even seem aware that Edward was walking beside him.

Edward turned his head and saw another soul on his other side. Then they were all around him, behind and ahead and on either side. They were everywhere, and they were all walking in the same direction.

There were souls of men, women, and children of all ages. They stared ahead with fixed and calm gazes. None looked around or made any noise. They walked side by side without seeming to notice the others walking next to them. They walked as one.

To Edward, it was all very disturbing. He stared at Fate's back, trying to take deep, calming breaths. But he could feel his heart racing, and his breaths were more like shallow gasps.

Edward didn't think he was bothering anyone, but he soon became aware of a disturbance among the souls. The one walking next to him moaned slightly and made agitated movements, which caused some of the others to do the same. Edward felt a panic, but he didn't know what to do.

Fate whispered softly, "It's your heartbeat. It's racing. And you're breathing. It's loud, and the souls can hear it. Because you're nervous and worried, the souls are feeling the same. They can sense your nerves, and that you are living. Just the fact if being alive among the dead can cause disturbance."

"What can I do?" Edward whispered.

"Try to calm down. They can't hurt you. If you remain calm and relaxed, they will follow suit."

Edward took another deep breath and felt his pulse slow down, but the souls still seemed restless to him.

He then saw Fate reach into her basket and drop something on the path. He realized they were petals, white lily petals. Fate started to sing in a clear, soprano voice. "Dead man, dead man, why do you follow me? I've no coins to lay on your eyes as you sleep. No bread or wine to offer you salvation. Dead man, dead man, why do I see you? Can you tell me from where you have traveled? Do you know where you go?"

The song was hauntingly beautiful. Edward could feel a calmness settle over the souls, and they continued to walk undisturbed.

He suddenly felt someone take his hand. He looked down at the soul of a little girl. She was holding on to his hand and swaying back and forth to the song. She was smiling. Fate stopped singing and stopped dropping the lily petals. She seemed unworried about the soul that had grasped Edward's hand.

"What should I do?" Edward asked. The little soul had stopped swaying but continued to smile as she walked next to him.

"Remain calm and let her hold your hand. She means no harm. Children's souls are much more attuned to human thoughts and feelings. She just wants someone to keep her company for a while. She'll let go in a bit."

"Okay." Edward glanced down at the smiling girl. She was a pretty little child. As she held his hand, he became aware of memories that weren't his. Of a mother's smiling face. Of summer days and games. Of childhood innocence. And of a river. Of being unable to swim. Of the unbearable urge to breathe underwater.

"Oh," Edward said thoughtfully as he realized the way the child had died.

The little girl looked up at him and grinned. "Pretty song."

"Yes, it was," Edward answered, surprised that she could talk.

"I'm going home," the soul said, skipping a little.

Images of clouds and light came to Edward's mind. "Yes. You're going home."

"You're silly!"

Edward smiled and squeezed her hand a little. "Yeah, I guess I am."

She giggled and let go of his hand to move ahead. Edward watched her until she disappeared from his view.

"Where are they going?" Edward whispered.

Fate shrugged. "Some go north, some go south. For now they travel the main road that will eventually split into two different paths. They will separate to walk the way they are destined."

"And they have no choice of where they walk?"

"All choices were made while they lived. The time for choices is past."

Edward shivered slightly. He asked, "Where does south lead?"

Fate turned to look at him. "Where do you think?"

Edward didn't answer, but he shuddered. Fate nodded. "Invidia Green knows the way very well. One would never want to go south, Edward. Know that."

Edward lowered his head in thought.

It was silent, Edward keeping pace with Fate. To him, his footsteps were awfully loud. None of the souls made any noises as they walked. Sound seemed to amplify here. The souls may have known he was alive, but they seemed to have accepted him. Either that or they were uninterested in him. But then he heard a chuckle. "You're a far way from home, aren't you, son?"

Edward turned to see an old man walking next to him. He looked almost like Santa Claus, with a long white beard and kind, faded-blue eyes. He was shorter than Edward and bigger.

Edward glanced at Fate. She had looked at them but then turned back to stare ahead, unconcerned with the fact that Edward seemed to be popular with the souls.

The old man chuckled again, a rich kind chuckle. "I could sense there was someone living here. Good lord, you're loud! Could hear your footsteps a mile away. And I thought to myself, what's a living person doing in the land of the dead? Must have some interesting story to tell. Seeing as how just walking on Dead Man's Path is downright boring, I thought I'd come and have a little talk with that person."

Edward looked up again at Fate in confusion. The old man said he could sense someone who was living—as in just one. Just what the hell was Fate anyway? Edward sighed a weary sigh, tired of trying to figure it all out.

He had almost forgotten about the old man by his side until he felt a tug on his sleeve. "Well, don't just ignore me, son."

"Oh, s-sorry," Edward stuttered, turning his attention to the soul. "Um … I guess I'm just not used to talking to souls."

The old man laughed. "No, I don't suppose you are. It's all right. Not like when I was alive I talked to dead people on a daily basis either. People would've thought I was crazy."

Edward smiled, sensing a kind heart in this man. The old man's hand still rested on his arm, and the soul's memories started to flow into Edward's mind. He accepted them without conflict, understanding now that there was no danger. There were considerably more memories from than this old man than from the little girl soul who had held his hand earlier. Mostly he saw a woman, someone the old man had loved a great deal. He saw her smiling face as it grew older, still beautiful in the old man's eyes. They were always together … until the end. Then he sensed a deep sadness from the old man, who had continued life without her. Edward felt the pain in his chest and shortness of breath of the old man's last day of living.

Edward nodded in understanding. Not questioning why the old man wanted Edward to see his memories, but accepting the responsibility without hesitation. The old man seemed satisfied and even grateful before finally dropping his hand away from Edward's arm.

The old man's mood turned serious then, and he asked, "Why are you here, son? You're not dead, and this isn't a place for the living."

"It's hard to explain."

"Let me see if I can help anyway. Old men like me know an awful lot of things."

Edward looked away from the old man's concerned face and answered, "I made a mistake. Someone I'm looking for is here. I need to make things right."

"Hmmm …" the old man said, rubbing his beard in thought. Edward knew the old man had done that a lot when he was alive. "That won't be an easy thing to do here. People who are here aren't really meant to leave here."

"I know."

The old man's face turned sympathetic as he stared up at Edward, but he nodded. "Responsibility for others can be a heavy burden to bear."

Edward lowered his head. "I'm the reason she's here. She is very important to me. I have to do this."

"I know, son. Just understand what you're getting into."

"I understand."

The old man nodded again and grinned. "Your friend is very lucky to have someone like you in her life."

"Thank you."

The old man patted Edward on the shoulder and said, "Take this advice, then, from an old dead man. Keep your eyes open, your back straight, and your mind clear. Protect those who are weaker than you. And know that even if you walk the road of night, you're heading toward the dawn."

Edward nodded. "I will … and thank you."

The old man stretched. "Well, I guess you're done listening to the crazy old dead man. Besides, my dawn is waiting for me."

"Yes. Find peace, old man," Edward answered.

The old man laughed as he walked on. "I plan to, son. Time for this old man to find his rest."

When the old man was gone, Edward felt a faint sense of loss. But he knew the old man was walking north; he'd be okay.

All that time, Fate hadn't said anything, but she remarked thoughtfully after the old man had gone, "The souls seem drawn to you, Edward. They must trust you."

Edward didn't reply. Fate fell silent again, leaving them to their thoughts. It seemed like a long time passed before Fate said, "We will leave the path to go our separate way. We cannot travel to where these souls go."

"Okay," Edward answered. Hearing Fate's voice jolted him a little. They had been walking on the path for a while now. Edward had no sense of time here, but he was becoming used to walking on the path. It put him in a trancelike state. Step after step, and watching Fate's back and the souls. It was strange, but the souls didn't bother him anymore. It was almost easy to walk beside them.

"This is our turn, Edward. Don't miss it, for one can't walk back on this path."

Edward saw the road leading off of the main path. "Got it. I'm ready."

They moved toward the side of the path. Edward was surprised to see that the souls got out of their way. It was almost like they could sense where Edward needed to go.

Edward glanced ahead and saw the little girl again. She was walking forward, but she had turned to look behind her. Edward grinned and gave a little wave. She giggled and waved back before continuing on.

"Turn off," Fate said. "Now."

Edward turned off of the path with Fate. It felt almost strange to leave it.

Fate looked up and asked, "Are you all right?"

"Yes."

"You did well. It's not easy to walk on Dead Man's Path. It's harder to leave it."

"I noticed," Edward agreed and gazed at the road that stretched ahead of them. "Is this the way to the garden?"

"Yes. The Forget-Me-Not Garden is this way."

The path was much smaller than Dead Man's Path. It was more like a trail. It led right through the woods. But at the end of this path was the garden, and Emily would be there. Edward straightened his back again in determination. He was almost there. He could sense Emily waiting for him.

I'm coming, Edward thought grimly.

Fate seemed to read his thoughts. She said seriously, "Let us continue then."

And together they started walking again. Ramona flew down to land on Edward's shoulder. Edward didn't even notice her weight or fear her long, sharp talons. Getting to Emily was the only thing that mattered.

Hang on, Emily. I'm coming.

The Grim Reaper

He knew the exact moment when Fate entered this world. He could sense her presence, smell her sweet scent. His Fate had come to his world. Another was with her. Edward Mikes had come for Emily Thorn.

The Grim Reaper had seen the love blossom between the two of them as they grew older. He could sense Edward's sheer determination to save Emily. Perhaps Edward would be strong enough, perhaps not. Either way, the Grim Reaper would be ready.

He was standing guard at the gates of the Forget-Me-Not Garden. His massive scythe rested by his side. He was aware that there had been a slight disturbance among the souls a while ago. He knew that Fate was perfectly capable of calming them and so he didn't worry about it. Soon enough he had felt a calmness settle over the souls again.

They were off the main path now. They were coming.

He had heard Edward's vow; he knew the strength of his will.

"Edward Mikes," the Grim Reaper said solemnly. "I can feel your determination. I know of your strength. Do you have what it takes to face me? All for her?"

CHAPTER SIX

The River of Forgotten

Fate

Fate ended up leaving the hometown where she and Zach had grown up. It wasn't a big town, and people started talking about her. Even her old friends stopped speaking to her. Not that she blamed them too much. After all, while everyone else grew older, Fate stayed the same. Nothing ever changed about her. Time passed, but it seemed to have forgotten about her.

Fate watched as her mother developed gray hairs and her father's skin wrinkled. All her friends grew older, got married, and had kids. Fate didn't look a day older than on the day of "the incident." That's what everyone called Zachary's sudden disappearance. Everyone looked at her strangely when she walked down the street, and no one made eye contact with her anymore.

So she left. Fate kissed her parents good-bye and told them she'd keep in touch. No one else in town would miss her. She had already left them behind.

Fate traveled for a while with no real destination in mind. She sort of stumbled across the carnival. The ringmaster didn't bat an eye when she asked to join. "What do you do?"

"I tell the future," she answered calmly.

"A fortune-teller, huh? Could use one of them. Everyone wants to know their futures."

"Yes. Sometimes it's better not to know, though," Fate couldn't help but say.

Something like sympathy came across his face. He nodded once. "You got secrets? Everyone here has secrets. You don't want to be judged? You won't be. Do your job. Keep your head down, and you're welcome to join my band of freaks."

The first few months were hard to adjust to. After all, how many people went from living normal lives to joining a traveling carnival? The carnies didn't warm up to her very fast, which was fine with her. She didn't want anything to do with people. She did her job, ate and slept, and counted down each agonizingly slow day until Halloween. Sometimes it shocked her to realize how detached she became from people … and life.

Fate felt that she was getting better at sensing him now. Sometimes she could make out his voice on the winds, or feel a cold sensation right next to her where he would be standing. She lived for those moments when she could tell that he was with her. But the more focused Fate was on sensing Zachary, the less aware of her surroundings she became. None of that mattered to her anymore. One night, that could have cost her dearly.

It was after hours, and Fate couldn't sleep. She often had trouble sleeping, and she was usually awake for long hours of the night. This night she decided to take a walk. She'd done it before, and the darkness held no fear for her.

The night was cold, and she walked under a starry sky. It was early October. Knowing it was nearing the time she'd be able to see Zachary made her heart beat faster. It was funny, but Fate didn't feel truly alive until she was with Zach. It was like being frozen and dormant inside, and seeing Zachary made everything start working again. Her heart remembered to beat, and she could breathe easier.

Fate was deep in her thoughts. It seemed like a harmless night as she wandered through the carnival. It took a long time for her to notice that someone was following her, until she heard the sound of his footsteps as he drew nearer.

Fate turned and saw the man. She couldn't remember his name, but she knew he worked at the carnival. She thought he helped with the animals. Fate had never bothered to learn much about her coworkers but she didn't like the looks of this man. He always smelled like cigar smoke and animals and alcohol. He was taller than her and strongly built. He had a dangerous look about him. Fate had caught him staring at her before. He was approaching her.

She shouldn't have gone outside.

"Aren't you up a little late, sugar? You looking for some company? I'd be happy to offer you mine," he said with a brown-toothed grin.

"No. I just needed some fresh air. But I'm heading back to my trailer now."

Fate started to walk around him, being careful not to get too close, but he blocked her way.

"Ah, don't be in such a rush, sugar."

"Move out of my way."

"You know, you shouldn't be so cold. I'm the only friend you got. No one else wants to be around you, considering how you think you're better than us."

"I don't think I'm better than any of you. I just want to be left alone. Please move out my way," Fate said, trying again to get past him. He blocked her again and moved closer.

"It's not often something so young and pretty shows up around here. You should be with me. I know how to treat women."

"No, thank you."

"See? There you go again, acting so cold."

She moved back too late. He lunged faster than she thought he could, latching on to her arm with a painful grip. She tried to pull away, but his hand tightened and she gasped in pain.

"I think you just need help warming up," he leered as he pulled her closer.

"Let go of me!" Fate yelled and jerked back, hitting him with her free arm.

He laughed. "You hit like a girl. I'm going to teach you how to behave."

Fate's heart skipped a beat. She used her nails to claw at his face. She heard a howl and was thrown back. She hit the ground hard as he stood over her screaming. "You bitch, you almost clawed my eye out! I'll make you pay! I swear I will!"

Fate saw him looming over. Part of his face was bloody, and the other part was twisted in rage. He drew back his fist. Fate closed her eyes, ready for the blow, but it never came. She felt a sudden chill of air and opened her eyes.

The man still stood over her, but he wasn't moving. He was completely still. His eyes were wide with shock and terror, his fist frozen in midair. Suddenly she heard a strange gurgling noise come from his throat, like he was choking on something. She saw the blood bubble out of his mouth. His shirt was stained with crimson that dripped on the ground. So much blood, and she had no idea how it happened.

The man's eyes seemed to rest on her face for the longest moment before he was roughly shoved to the side. He fell to the ground dead … and Fate saw Zachary standing behind him. He was lowering his scythe to his side. His face was hard and angry as his gaze fell to Fate on the ground.

"Zachary," Fate breathed.

Once Zachary had assessed her condition, he said in a grim voice, "Never touch what belongs to me."

Fate didn't understand what he meant until she looked again at the dead man's body and saw his soul standing over it. His expression was one of confusion and fear. Fate gasped and scooted away. She managed to stand on shaky legs and ran behind Zachary.

"Don't be afraid, Fate. He can no longer harm you," Zachary said. "Neil Samson, your time on this earth has passed. Join the others on the path. I will follow shortly."

Neil's soul was shaking with fear, but he had to obey the Grim Reaper's orders. He nodded, and his soul vanished. Once he was gone, Zachary turned back to Fate.

"Zachary, I'm sorry," Fate tried to say, choking on her sobs, but Zach shook his head.

"His time was drawing near. I would have come for him tomorrow anyway, from an accident with the horses. However, I will allow no one to harm you, Fate. You are mine."

"Yes, I am. I love you," Fate answered. She moved to place her hand on his ice-cold cheek.

Zachary turned his face to her hand and seemed to breathe her in. He placed a cold kiss on her palm, then took her hand gently in his. "I will take you back to your trailer. Then we must part. I cannot stay."

Fate nodded and let him lead her back, never wanting to let him go. She was shaken up from everything that happened, her stomach like ice and her legs like jelly. She didn't know if she would make it, if she could continue to walk. Everything became foggy.

"Zach," Fate whispered, and suddenly she was in his arms. Her head rested against his shoulder. They were still a distance from her trailer, but in just a moment Zach was laying her down on her bed. Her shoes were gone and he was covering her with a blanket. Her eyes stared into his. He bent and kissed her forehead, then stood.

"Wait …" Fate whispered, tears pooling in her eyes and rolling down her cheeks.

"Wait for me. It will not be long before we are together again."

"Yes." Fate sighed, knowing she would have to let him go for now.

"Be careful when you go for evening walks. Do not stray far from your trailer," Zachary ordered.

"Yes. I will, Zach. I love you."

"I love you too, Fate. Get some rest."

Fate could feel herself become drowsy, and she blinked. One moment Zachary was there, and then when she opened her eyes, he was gone.

No one knew who killed Neil Samson. The ringmaster assumed it had something to do with Neil's shady past. Perhaps an old enemy had finally come to take his revenge. It was no great loss. The show must go on.

Edward

"Fate?"

"Yes?"

"I was wondering about something. Why is it Halloween night that we can come here? What's special about tonight?"

"Oh, right. I never explained that part to you, did I? To put it simply, on All Hallows' Eve the living remember the dead. Some believe that on All Souls Day the living and the dead are connected again, and though the dead can never return to the living, there is a sort of bridge that opens—the portal that we passed through. The living remember those who have departed. They pray for them, have memories of them. The ones who have passed and left someone behind can feel their memories, hear their prayers. It soothes them, lulls them. It enables us to walk beside them. Does that make sense?"

"About as much as everything else that's happened tonight." Edward sighed, running his hand through his hair.

Fate laughed, and Edward grinned as they continued on. Ramona still perched on his shoulder. Edward had grown used to the three of them together. It was most certainly an odd company, but it was one with a purpose. And Edward hadn't forgotten his purpose for being here.

Fate said thoughtfully, "You know, All Hallows' Eve is also the day the Grim Reaper can return to the world of the living."

Edward stopped to stare at Fate in surprise. Fate stopped too and turned to look at him. Her long black hair fell around her face. Her eyes were too wise for her age.

"So … what, he gets a day off or something?"

"Um, sort of. I guess that's right. It's a night when the souls can go unguarded because they are at peace with the prayers and the memories. Being remembered lulls a soul when it walks. The Grim Reaper is able to leave them for a little while."

"But why would he?" Edward asked.

Fate looked down to the ground and answered, "To be with someone. Someone he loves."

"Oh," Edward sighed, understanding. Fate still didn't look at him. He ran his hand through his hair again and asked, "And that person he loves would still be alive after all this time?"

"Yes," Fate answered.

"But not tonight?"

"No. If the living is in the land of the dead, he cannot leave. He has to remain to maintain balance."

Edward was quiet for a moment before he said, "It must be hard for him … and for the person he was going to see."

Fate didn't answer, and Edward asked no more questions. They continued on. But after a while Fate said quietly, "Edward, we aren't far from the garden now. The

Grim Reaper will be guarding the gates. You will need be ready to face him."

"How?" Edward asked.

"You are still willing? After everything you've seen, you still want to challenge the Grim Reaper?"

"Yes," Edward answered without hesitation. "Emily is waiting for me. Please show me what I need to do."

Fate sighed but answered wearily, "To enter the Forget-Me-Not Garden, you will have to fight the Grim Reaper and win. You will need a weapon."

Edward had no idea how he would be able to defeat death itself, but he knew he would have to win. "Where can I find a weapon?"

"I will show you—but know this. It won't be easy."

"Okay," Edward answered.

They were rounding a bend. Edward thought he heard the sound of running water. It was dark enough here that Edward couldn't see any yet, but as they walked farther, he was sure that's what he heard.

Then he saw a bridge. Under it ran a river. It wasn't very wide, but he saw that it ran very deep. He couldn't see the bottom. It ran fast as well. To Edward it looked like any other river, but something about it didn't feel right. It made his muscles tense and his stomach twist. There was just something ominous about it. He didn't want to go onto the bridge over it.

But Fate stopped beside the river to stare down into its depth. Edward wanted to call out to her to stay away from the water, but then who would know more about it than her? In fact, Edward noticed, this world held no terror for Fate at all.

Fate turned to Edward and smiled encouragingly. "It's okay. Please come here."

Edward hadn't even realized that he had stopped walking. He was just standing there, staring at her. *Coward,* Edward thought, angry at himself for being so weak, and walked up to Fate. Ramona hooted once and flew off his shoulder to a tree branch. She watched them with her wise round eyes.

The closer to the river Edward got, the more afraid he became. Sweat started to bead out on his forehead, and he could feel his heart beating frantically. Was it just him, or did it seem there was some sort of sound coming from the river? Almost like fearful murmurs. *Damn it. I have not come all this way just to be frightened off by a stupid river.*

"Edward, relax. It's natural to be afraid here," Fate said reassuringly as he finally came to stand next to her. "After all," she continued, turning to the river, "this river contains fears and sorrows."

"What?"

"As you've already seen, the souls walk on Dead Man's Path as one. At some point, they will part ways to go where they will spend eternity."

"Yes, I understand that," Edward answered.

"For those who travel south, don't you think they should fear where they go? Or don't you think the souls would mourn the living just as the living mourn the dead?"

"I … guess so."

"This river has a name. It's called the River of Forgotten. This is where their emotions go," Fate explained, looking up at him again. "For souls to travel undisturbed on the path, they have to be without fear and sorrow. This river is flowing with everyone's memories of life. It's no wonder you are afraid to approach it."

Edward nodded and cautiously approached the river. It was true that he could hear voices coming from it. It was some sort of muttering, like scared whispers or choked sobs.

He was almost afraid to ask, but Edward was no coward. "Fate," he said quietly, "what must I do here?"

Fate looked at him apologetically. "This is where you must find your weapon. It is hidden in this river's depths. You must submerge yourself in the river and find it."

Somehow Edward had known that, one way or the other, he'd end up in that damn river. But still the thought of diving into that water sent dread and fear through him. The river was so inky black, he had no idea how he would find the weapon. "How will I see it?"

"It will appear to you as a light."

Edward stepped closer to the river so that his shoe was right on the edge of it. He stared down into the water and said, "It looks so deep."

"The River of Forgotten has no bottom. It runs without end," Fate replied. Seeing Edward's visible fear, she went on, "It's okay. Memories can't hurt you. However, know that your fears rest in the river as well, now that you have entered the land of the dead. To find your weapon, you will have to face your own fears. Find your light within the darkness."

"My light?" Edward asked faintly. The river seemed to lap toward him as if sensing his presence and waiting for him to enter its unfathomable depths. *Come, Edward,* it challenged, and Edward could feel his knees growing weak with fear.

Fate said softly, "You don't have to do this, Edward. You don't have to jump into that water."

Hearing Fate snapped Edward out of his trance, reminding him that he wasn't alone. He answered her in a grim, hard voice, "Yes, I do."

"Do you?"

"Don't you see?" Edward turned toward Fate then. "Not saving Emily is my biggest fear. The thought of living life without her. Of her being here forever, all because I couldn't protect her. That is unimaginable to me. Unacceptable. So if I fail, to me, *I'd* be unacceptable."

"Edward," Fate whispered. Tears formed in her eyes.

"Please don't cry, Fate," Edward suddenly said with a grin. "I'll be fine." He waited for Fate to smile and nod; then he turned back to the river. His smile turned into a hard line of determination. "I will find my weapon. I will win against the Grim Reaper. I will save Emily," he vowed to the river and to himself. An image of Emily's smiling face flashed into his mind, and his hand clenched. *Emily.* And he jumped into the icy black water without a second thought.

The water swallowed him. Edward felt himself sinking into the depths. The fearful whispering grew louder. He could sense endless amounts of people's fears. He heard everything from a child's sobbing to women's screams and men's cries of pain. But no matter where he turned his head, he couldn't see anything though the inky-black water.

Then Edward's own memories started to fill his head: every memory he had that had ever caused him fear. Mostly he saw his dad. Heard his yelling. Remembered how his head hurt after his dad struck him. He remembered being afraid for his mother, worried he would never be strong enough to protect her.

Then his dad died, and new fears became apparent to him. He remembered that feeling of loss and not understanding why he felt so alone. Edward remembered seeing his mom crying and wondering how he would be able to keep them going. He remembered the guilt he felt, wondering if his dad died because Edward hadn't tried hard enough to save him.

He moved to cover his ears with his hands as the countless memories surrounded him. He feared he would be consumed as the river carried him whichever way it wanted. Edward didn't know if he was up or down anymore. Everything around him was utterly black.

They were standing outside their school. After spending the day avoiding Emily, she had finally caught him when he was making a dash for home. After his father died, Edward couldn't bring himself to talk to anyone about how he felt. He knew he was hurting Emily by not talking to her, but he couldn't face her.

Edward was doing a good job of avoiding her during school. Everyone else gave him the space he needed, but Emily was different. She always knew how to get through his defenses.

He could hear Emily calling after him as he was walking away. Coward, he called himself, but he kept walking. He stopped when he felt Emily grab a fistful of his shirt.

"Please, Ed. Talk to me," Emily pleaded softly, clutching tightly at his shirt, afraid to let go.

"It's my fault. It's because I wasn't strong enough," Edward said gruffly, refusing to turn and look at her.

"There you go again. Always taking on more than you should," Emily said sadly.

"You know it's true, Emily. My dad is dead. And it's my fault. I wasn't strong enough to keep my family going. I wasn't strong enough to keep him alive."

"No. Your family's still going because of you. You can't take responsibility for something your father did to himself. It's not your fault."

Edward's head dropped. He drew in a ragged breath and whispered hoarsely, "Just give up on me. I'm afraid I'll end up like him. You know it too. You should move on."

He felt Emily bury her face in his back. "How much longer are you going to beat yourself up over this? You're not your dad, Edward. You never will be like him. So stop running away from me. Please. I need you."

Edward finally turned to look at Emily's tear-streaked face. "How could you ever ask me to give up on you?" she went on. "When you are the one who kept me going after my mom died? You're so strong, Edward. And you always take on too much responsibility. I know that I'm a burden to you. But I can't let you go. I need you."

Edward took Emily in his arms. "You are never a burden to me," he said, holding her to him.

"I always depend on you."

"I don't mind."

"But I thought," Emily continued, "that you could depend on me too. I could be there for you. But you have to let me in. The two of us together. We kind of balance each other out, don't we?"

"Yes," Edward answered.

"Please, Edward. Just don't run away from me anymore. I want to help you. I want to be with you. Promise me you'll stay with me."

After a moment, Edward sighed and said, "I promise. I won't run away anymore. I'll stay with you, Emily."

"And promise me that you'll stop blaming yourself for your dad's death. And that you'll stop worrying you'll turn out like him."

A long pause passed between them. Emily looked up at Edward's hard face. "You're different from him. You're strong. You'll never be like him. Promise me that you'll never forget that."

"I promise," Edward finally said, giving in and holding her closer.

She wrapped her arms around his neck and buried her against him. "And I promise I'll be there for you. And I won't be a burden to you."

"You could never be a burden to me. You mean more to me than you could ever know. I promise that I will always be there to protect you. Always."

Emily smiled up into his face. "Always taking on more than you should. You know I love you, Edward."

"I love you too, Emily. I always have and always will."

Emily. Edward's eyes snapped opened and narrowed. *I will save you.* He was still floating under the water, but now he had a sense of direction. Now that he had found his resolve to face his greatest fears, he could see though the darkness.

Show me what I need to find, Edward commanded the river.

The river seemed to quiver around him, and in its depths he saw the light. He swam toward it, moving easily through the water as it no longer held fear for him. The river sensed this and offered no resistance. It settled down as if resting.

Edward reached out a hand as he neared the light. For a moment, he saw Emily. She was floating beneath the water with him. His eyes widened and he struggled to reach her faster. She was smiling at him, that smile that was so sweet and just for him. Her beautiful ash-blond hair swirled around her face. She reached out a hand for him. *Emily.*

But she was gone when he touched her. *No,* Edward moaned silently. She was gone in the blink of an eye, just like before. Seeing her and then losing her again hurt like hell, like a knife in his chest had been viciously twisted. Edward closed his eyes and clenched his hand into a fist.

That was when he realized something was in his hand. He opened his eyes again and saw that he was holding a weapon. It was a massive scythe. The blade looked like it could cut anything in half with just one hit. It looked like something the Grim Reaper would carry.

Edward pondered his weapon for a moment and then swam toward the surface, moving easily through the icy black water. He saw Fate standing at the river's edge, staring down at him. She looked worried. He broke through the surface. Fate ran up to him as he pulled himself onto the bank.

"Edward, are you all right?"

"Yeah," Edward answered. He pulled his scythe from the water behind him. He heard Fate gasp as he brought his weapon to his side. It was heavy now that it was out of the water.

"It appears that you found your light within the darkness," Fate whispered.

"Yeah. It was Emily," Edward said with a faint smile. "She was the light that guided me."

"That's good."

"Fate," Edward said grimly, still not looking at her. "I think it's time I asked you again. How old are you?"

Silence filled the air. Edward stared down at his weapon and waited. Finally he heard a soft sigh. "Have you figured out everything then?"

"Just about," Edward affirmed, standing and looking down at Fate. Her eyes showed again a knowledge too great for her age and a sadness that wasn't understandable. "You're the one the Reaper would have gone to see tonight, right? If it weren't for Emily and me?"

"Yes."

"Because you love him. And he loves you."

"Yes. The Grim Reaper used to be Zachary Conner. When he was alive, we were a couple. We were going to get married someday, but then …"

"He paid the price," Edward finished for her when she stopped.

"Yes. He paid the price to save me. The price is to take the place of the Grim Reaper. You can't just come here and return a soul to the living. Whether that soul is living or dead, it must remain here. Only the Grim Reaper may return a soul to its body, and it has to be someone that he loves."

Edward just stared at her. Fate's eyes filled with tears. She looked away and whispered, "I'm so sorry, Edward. You must hate me."

"No."

"What?"

"I don't hate you, Fate. I am forever in your debt."

Fate dared to look up at him and saw that Edward was smiling gently down at her. "How can you say that?"

"Without you, I never would have been able to find my way here. To Emily."

"Edward, don't you understand? To save Emily, you will have to defeat the Grim Reaper and take his place. Forever."

"I understand."

"And you're okay with that? You're willing to give up your soul and spend the rest of eternity reaping from the living? Never resting? Never living again? That is what you must do to save Emily."

"I know." Edward's expression was absolutely serious. "I've already told you, I will do whatever I have to to save Emily. My soul for hers. It's not even a contest for me."

"The responsibility of the Grim Reaper is a heavy burden to bear."

The smile back, Edward answered, "Emily always said I take on too much responsibility. But I'm kind of used to it. So I guess if anyone is qualified for this job, I'm the man."

Fate just stared at him in shock. Finally she giggled. "Edward Mikes, you are something else. You just never stop surprising me."

"I shouldn't surprise you too much. After all, Zachary Conner did what I'm about to do. He was willing to risk everything to save you too."

"Yes, he was," Fate said sadly, but still smiling. "Zach was a lot like you. Serious, determined, and maybe just a little stubborn."

Edward laughed and said with a shrug, "I guess that does sound like me. That's what everyone describes me as, anyway."

"It's a compliment. I always loved Zach. I always will. And even though Zachary is different, I know he loves me too."

"How is he different?"

"He's a shadow of his former self. He doesn't laugh anymore. I never would have thought it possible, but he is much more serious and quiet now than when he was alive. He's told me that I hold his humanity within me. And maybe that's true, because we are bonded in ways that no living human can ever be bound to another. But … that's fine, because my love for Zachary goes past life and death. He gave his soul to save me, and I will wait for him for however long that takes."

"How long …"

"Zachary became the Grim Reaper in the year 1850. He was twenty, and I had just turned seventeen." Fate smiled at Edward's look of disbelief. "We grew up in Chicago. Wasn't near as big as it is today, but it always was a beautiful place. He was a hard worker. He built houses back then. Even before we started courting, I had always loved him. I found that he felt the same way about me. When he starting seeing me, it was the best feeling in the world for me. I thought we would have a long and happy life together."

Edward frowned and asked, "And then?"

Fate's eyes hardened. "And then Envy."

"Envy? He separated you too?" Edward asked, surprised.

"Yes. Zachary wanted to marry me, but whether for lack of money or status, he didn't feel that he could. I tried to tell him that none of that mattered to me. The only thing I ever wanted in life was him."

Edward placed his hand on her shoulder when he saw the tears. Fate put her hand over his. It was so fragile looking.

Fate started walking again, and Edward automatically followed. They walked over the bridge.

"He took me out to a potluck that night. He looked so handsome. Sitting next to him, I thought I was the luckiest woman in the world. And when he was walking me back to my home, he took my hand and told me he loved me. He said that no mattered what, he'd find a way to provide for me, to give me everything I could ever want. And I told him again that as long as he was in my life, nothing else mattered to me.

"It was All Hallows' Eve. It was dark and it was cold. And for some reason I was nervous. Then I remember seeing *him*. Envy was leaning against the wall in an alley. He was waiting for us, of course. He called out to us. He offered a deal that Zachary couldn't refuse. And Zachary lost."

Edward lowered his head in shame, knowing he had done the same thing to Emily. She was here without him because he had failed to realize the danger. He had failed to protect her. *Unforgivable,* Edward thought.

But Fate kept talking, unaware of Edward's inner conflict. "I don't remember much after that. What I do remember is very foggy. I don't know how Zachary found his way to me or who the previous Reaper was. I remember very clearly opening my eyes after sleeping and seeing Zachary standing there. Just like that, there he was. Zachary was ghostly pale, very haggard looking, and he had several injuries that looked fatal. But they started to heal until they disappeared completely. I remember throwing my arms around him and letting him lift me up. He kept telling me he was sorry. And he took me home."

Edward walked silently behind her, listening to her story. "And then what happened?"

"I waited. I'm still waiting, I guess. Every year that I live, I wait for Zach to come back to me. One night a year on Halloween.

"That next day after he returned me home, no one could find Zachary Conner. After searching for him for a few days, they claimed him dead by accident. I was in no shape to explain anything, and they would have thought I was crazy anyway. Even I thought I was crazy. I wanted to see Zach so much that it hurt. The only thing that kept me sane was his promise that he would come back to me in a year. And he did.

"I was better then. Knowing I would see him was enough for me. But I never grew older. When all my friends and family aged without me, I knew I had to leave. I started traveling, and it was by chance I joined the carnival."

"Did you know Envy was at the carnival?"

"No. I didn't realize it until after I found you. Just as well. I would have tried to go after the bastard." Fate gave a little laugh then. "The Grim Reaper would have had to save me all over again."

"How? I thought he couldn't see you until Halloween night."

"It's been so many years now that we're very much attuned to one another. Sometimes I hear his voice in the wind. Or I'll see flashes of him next to me. I live for those moments. But if I'm in danger, he comes in person. He won't let anything happen to me. And who could ever win against death?"

Edward stopped then and so did Fate. She turned to Edward and seemed to see the grim despair in his eyes. Fate bit her lip and said softly, "Sorry, Edward. I didn't mean that."

"I know. It's okay. I know it'll be near impossible to defeat the Grim Reaper. But somehow I'll find a way to do it."

"It can be done. Zachary found a way, and so can you."

"But what will happen to you if I win? What will happen to the Grim Reaper?"

"Zachary and I will finally be at peace. We'll be able to move on from this world. It's the one thing a Reaper wants more than anything—to be with his loved ones in the next world. To rest. If you defeat Zachary, then you will be giving him the most important gift you could ever give him: an honorable death and the permission to rest in peace. Him and me too."

Edward was quiet for a moment. Then he asked, "That's what you want, Fate? To die with Zachary?"

Fate laughed softly. "Don't you understand? Zachary and I are already dead. We stopped living more than a hundred years ago. Seeing Zach every year has kept me going, but I am weary of this world. I long for rest. To be with Zachary forever. More than anything, I want Zach to be at peace. But I can't give him that, Edward. The only one who can is you."

"I'll try as hard as I can. I'd be happy to help you two. But you already know why I'm here. To get Emily. I will do anything in my power to protect her."

"I know," Fate answered with a smile. "And that's why I believe you will win. Because your love for Emily will give you the strength you need."

"My light within the darkness," Edward said thoughtfully. "I know what that is. It's Emily."

"Well done, Edward."

They continued on. Edward carried his scythe with determination, not sure what to expect, but knowing that it wouldn't change a damn thing. He was going to save Emily.

They rounded a last turn and the woods were left behind. Edward looked up in surprise at the openness, and he saw the gates. They were huge, standing proudly against the darkness of the sky. His breathing quickened as saw the name engraved in the iron: Forget-Me-Not Garden. He hadn't realized he'd stopped to stare until he heard Fate's voice beside him. "We're here. It's just up ahead."

"I see," Edward answered. He sounded breathless, but then so did Fate. This was it. They had finally made it.

And Edward could see that there was someone standing at the gates, a dark and silent guard. Someone, Edward knew, who had more power than anyone alive. Because that's what he took—life.

CHAPTER SEVEN

The Battle

Edward

"*Do you know what my favorite flower is, Ed?*"
Edward started walking forward. For once
Fate was following him. He could hear her slight breathing
from behind him, but he didn't dare look at her. His eyes
were focused on the guard, the Grim Reaper. Edward had
never seen him, of course, but who else could the dark figure
be?

The Reaper gave no notice that he was even aware of
Edward's approach, but Edward wasn't fooled. They were in
the Reaper's world, after all, and he was aware of everything
that went on in it.

Edward knew that this was Zachary Conner, or used to
be. He knew that Zachary hadn't chosen this for him or for
Fate. But Edward couldn't help but view him as the enemy.
The Grim Reaper was the only thing standing between him

and Emily. And didn't every mortal tend to view death as an enemy? The one nobody would ever win against.

"Well, what is it, then, silly?"

"I know. It's the forget-me-not. How could I forget?"

Ever since finding his weapon in the River of Forgotten, Edward had been hearing Emily's voice more frequently. He saw her too, standing on the path ahead of him, always gone before he could reach her. Always looking over her shoulder, smiling at him. Walking beside him through the woods. Only Ramona looked too, as if she could see Emily from her accustomed perch on Edward's shoulder. Edward didn't think he was going crazy. He knew he was getting closer, and the more he saw Emily, the more he quickened his pace.

For a moment Edward forgot where he was walking, until he felt Fate and grab hold of his shirt from behind. "Wait, Edward," she whispered.

Edward glanced behind, concerned about her, but Fate wasn't looking at him. She only had eyes for Zach, and they were filling with tears. Edward looked at the Grim Reaper too and was surprised to see how much closer he was to the gates and to the guard. That's why Fate had stopped him. *Fool,* Edward thought angrily. He could have walked right up to the Grim Reaper without realizing it, and then it would have been all over.

But the Grim Reaper still hadn't moved from his spot. He stood like a statue with his scythe by his side. He held it with only one hand, which surprised Edward. He had to carry his with both hands and still had trouble with the weight of it.

Edward wasn't sure what he had expected the Grim Reaper to look like—perhaps a bony skeleton with a skull face, wearing a dark cloak. He had the cloak right. That was it.

The Grim Reaper still looked like a man, only different. He was tall and strongly built, but his skin was so pale that Edward could almost see through him. The man's body shifted without the Reaper actually moving a muscle, almost as if the wind shifted through his body, making it move. Like they were one. *They probably are*, Edward thought with a chill.

"Well, Edward. You finally made it," the Grim Reaper finally said, making Edward flinch. His voice was calm and icy, which was more fearful then if he were yelling.

"You know my name?" Edward asked, and to his surprise he sounded calm and collected as well.

"I do."

"And you know why I've come?"

"Yes. You have come for Emily Thorn." The Grim Reaper's face was hard and emotionless. "The girl was taken from you in the land of living, and so you followed her here to the land of the dead. You wish her back. Isn't that right?"

"Yes. Is Emily in there?" Edward asked, looking toward the garden beyond the gates.

"Yes. Emily lies asleep in the garden."

"Then I'm going in to get her," Edward said with narrowing eyes.

"You are aware of the toll?"

"I am," Edward answered in an equally hard voice. "I am willing to give up my soul in exchange for hers and then defeat you. Then I will become the new Grim Reaper."

To Edward's surprise, he saw a ghost of a smile flash across the Reaper's face. He turned toward Fate. "He certainly is well informed, Fate."

Fate smiled, although a tear was sliding down her cheek. "Edward had already figured most of it out anyway. I only confirmed his statements. He is a smart man."

"Yes, and he has a strong soul. However ..." The Reaper trailed off, lowering his eyes.

Edward didn't know what to make of it. "I'm willing to give up my soul for Emily."

"I know that, Edward Mikes. You would not have made this journey if you weren't. What mortal would walk through the land of the dead if he weren't willing to risk everything? Emily means the world to you. I understand that. But being willing to become the Grim Reaper is not enough. You must be strong."

Edward straightened his back. "I'm strong enough."

"A fight against death itself is a battle beyond comprehension. You clearly aren't prepared. Look how you carry your weapon."

Edward glanced at his scythe. The blade was resting on the ground. Because of its weight, he had to set it down for a moment. He still held the rod firmly in his hands, but it took all of his strength just to carry the weapon. How would he be able to battle with it?

The Grim Reaper continued, "Do you believe you could possibly win against me when you can't even lift your weapon without struggle?"

"I'll manage," Edward replied. He had to. Emily was waiting for him.

The Grim Reaper nodded slightly. "Be warned. This is not a battle your body can withstand. You may turn back now if you choose."

"There is no going back for me."

"Then you wish to battle me? Answer carefully, Edward, for once we start, there is no stopping. It will be a battle to the death, and you will be fighting against death."

Edward closed his eyes and inhaled slowly. All the events that had happened to him in such a short period of time came rushing back. He felt as though he had lived far beyond his years already, and he knew he was a different man now from who he'd been yesterday. He was weary. What he was facing now was beyond understanding. He would never see his mother again. He would never return home. The only thing he could hope to do was take Emily home to Old Dave and pray that someday she would be able to forgive him for what he had done to her.

And Edward allowed himself to admit it … he was afraid.

"*Ed?*" an uncertain voice asked. A voice he would know anywhere. She was waiting for him.

"*It's okay, Emily. I promised. I will protect you.*"

Edward exhaled and opened his eyes. The Grim Reaper stood where he had been, waiting patiently. "I will fight you."

"I see," the Grim Reaper answered gravely. "Then prepare yourself."

Edward felt a pat on his shoulder. He turned to see Fate. She smiled up at him, and Edward returned the smile. Then she moved away to stand silently on the sideline. Her expression was one of worry.

Edward moved to stand a few paces from the Grim Reaper. He had managed to lift his blade again, although it took all of his strength to hold the weight of it. They stood face-to-face. "Tell me something, Zachary," Edward called out. The Grim Reaper didn't answer but raised his eyebrows in question. "What is it like to be death? Is it ... like an endless road of night?"

"No," Zachary answered, his voice sounding almost normal. He looked toward Fate, who was staring at him with undying love in her eyes. "It's like walking a road to the dawn."

"I understand," Edward said gruffly.

The Grim Reaper turned toward him, any human emotion vanishing completely. His eyes were darkness itself, void of any feeling. "Are you ready?"

Edward squared his shoulders and clenched his fists over the handle of his weapon. He could do this. He had to. "Yes."

He heard a sudden swish before he felt anything. And then he did feel it: a sharp, burning pain that took his breath away. Confused, he glanced down at his abdomen. A huge, clean strip had been cut deep into his stomach. He saw the blood ooze into the wound before gushing out in an uncontrolled wave. His knees almost gave out from under him.

Edward looked up at the Grim Reaper. The Reaper stood where he had been a second ago, but he was lowering his scythe to rest at his side. He was watching Edward with an almost bored expression.

What's going on? Where did this wound come from? Did he cut me? Edward asked himself, his eyes widening with shock.

There was something dripping from the Grim Reaper's scythe. It was blood. Edward hadn't even seen the Reaper move. His breathing quickened in fear.

This time the Grim Reaper lifted his blade in warning to Edward. *He's coming again,* Edward thought and raised his own scythe to defend himself. This time he saw the Reaper coming, but barely. He moved like a silent shadow, there one second and gone the next. He was so fast.

Another swoosh of air. Another agonizing, burning pain, this time on his left shoulder. He saw the blood running down his arm and onto his hands that clasped the handle. It made holding the weapon even more difficult because it was slick now. But Edward didn't have time to think about that. Another blow from his right side sent him flying. He landed with a thud and lay there for a moment, stunned. Blood was pooling on the ground around him. His whole body burned and hurt.

He's too fast. How can I fight him if I can't see him coming?

"On your feet, Edward."

Edward looked up at the Grim Reaper standing over him. He had never heard him approach. Edward stared in shock.

"We are not done yet," the Grim Reaper finished calmly.

"No, we're not," Edward said in return. His voice was hoarse and ragged, but calm at the same time. No matter what, Edward would not go down without a fight.

The Grim Reaper nodded and waited for Edward to regain his footing. Edward stumbled back a little and raised his own scythe. Streams of blood were running down his arms and body. Edward was strong, and he had been in fights before. His own father had once told him that in a fight, a man didn't care about rules. A man did whatever was necessary to win. Edward had never dreamed he would take his father's words to heart.

Edward charged the Grim Reaper, drawing his weapon back and bringing it forward, hoping to catch him off guard. He aimed for the Reaper's middle.

A blinding pain scorched his back. Edward fell forward, landing on his knees. The Grim Reaper stood behind him. Edward would have sworn he had never taken his eyes off him for a second. How did the Reaper get behind him? He heard Fate whimper from the side, but he didn't dare look at her.

"Damn it," Edward cursed. He got back to his feet and charged again. Anger, pain, and fear gave him the strength to keep moving. Adrenaline shot through his veins and pumped in his ears. He tried to forget the pain and the fact that he was losing too much blood.

Again and again he felt the searing pain of the Reaper's blade. Each time Edward fell, it became harder to rise. Each time the Grim Reaper patiently waited for him to stand again. Edward's blood was everywhere, and he had long since lost track of his injuries. He only knew that there were a lot.

Edward was once again sent flying. He struggled to a standing position. His breathing came in short and rapid gasps. His couldn't straighten his back and stood hunched over. He looked at the Grim Reaper and saw him fading as Edward tried to focus on him. Edward's vision was getting blurry. *Don't you dare pass out,* he thought angrily. He was so dizzy, and the earth seemed to tilt. He wasn't ashamed to admit it: he was afraid.

"*Damn it, I'm going to lose,*" Edward thought and closed his eyes for a moment.

"*That's a lot of blood.*"

Edward's eyes snapped open and he saw Emily standing next to him. Her expression was full of concern and sorrow. Edward didn't know this time if he was imagining her there or not. Maybe the Reaper and Fate could see her as well. But she was there to him, clear as day. Lovely as she had always been.

"Emily."

"*You don't have to do this, you know. You don't have to save me. You'll always be my hero. But it wasn't hard for me to die. And I don't want you to get hurt anymore. Please, Edward.*"

"I have to save you. It's my fault you're here."

Emily stared up at him. So pale and fragile. But her eyes burned with a fierce love, and it was only for Edward. "*Just let it go. It's okay to let me go. I don't want to be a burden to you anymore. You don't have to win. You don't have to fight for me. Just don't get hurt anymore. I can't bear it.*"

Edward stared at Emily for a moment, and then he smiled. He straightened his back until he was standing tall. Emily knew that pose, and she shook her head at him. But Edward remembered what to say.

"You could never be a burden to me, Emily. You mean more to me than you could ever know. And I promise that I will always be there to protect you. Always."

Emily lowered her head, but Edward saw her smile. It was sad, but it was as sweet as always. "*Always so stubborn. Always taking on more then you should. You know I love you, Edward.*"

"I love you too, Emily. I always have and always will."

"Edward. It's time to give up. You cannot win against me."

Edward wasn't looking at the Grim Reaper when he answered. He had eyes only for Emily. "I'm not done yet."

Emily nodded and smiled. Then she turned into a light and disappeared into Edward's blade. His whole scythe seemed to glow. It was suddenly weightless. Edward didn't need two hands to hold it anymore.

"We kind of balance each other out, don't we?"

"Yes, Emily. We do," Edward answered and lunged at the Grim Reaper.

He must have finally caught the Grim Reaper off guard, for he saw the flash of surprise in the coal-black eyes before the cloaked figure moved out of range. But Edward could follow his movements much more easily now. Edward was moving faster too, and he brought his scythe down in a wide arc.

For once the Grim Reaper was forced to raise his weapon in defense. The sound of the two blades clashing was like thunder in a raging storm. A faint smile passed over the Grim Reaper's mouth. "Well, Edward. It seems that you have improved."

Edward returned the smile. "Yeah. Sorry it took so long. But I found my light within the darkness, and it's given me the resolve to finish you."

"The light within the darkness. A most powerful weapon indeed. Face me then, Edward Mikes!" And with a sudden battle cry so unlike the usually silent Reaper, he lunged at Edward, wielding his massive blade like a true master.

Edward returned the battle cry. The two warriors faced off in a fight to the death, the kind which no mortal could ever survive. Edward wasn't sure when he had stopped being a mortal. He didn't care. He only wanted to win.

The blades of the scythes created lightning when they struck against one another, and the sound was enough to made Fate cover her ears and whimper in fear. To Fate, it was like watching two shadows moving too fast to follow.

The battle seemed to last forever. Edward fought strongly, but mortal now or not, he was still wounded badly and it was starting to slow him down. His breathing was rapid and sweat and blood poured down his face. The Reaper too was starting to labor, but he was in much better condition than Edward, and he already had the upper hand in wielding the scythe.

They broke off, neither of their blades striking flesh, and fell back. Edward took in deep breaths, trying to breathe this too-heavy air.

But suddenly the Grim Reaper was there again. Edward barely had time to defend himself. The sound of the two scythes boomed in his ears. The Grim Reaper stared at him over the crossed blades with hard, cold eyes. He pushed harder, and the Grim Reaper's blade came closer to Edward's face. "Why don't you give up, Edward? What drives you to fight me? Are you so determined to save Emily? It's your fault she's in here in the first place, where she will sleep forever in oblivion."

"Damn it," Edward whispered angrily as adrenaline pumped through him. "Don't you think I know that? That's the reason why *I will save her*!"

Edward broke loose and attacked the Grim Reaper with renewed strength. Edward swung his blade easily and again and again lunged at him. "Whatever it takes, I will save Emily!"

The Grim Reaper was on the defensive, but he wasn't outdone yet. He returned the attack, but Edward wouldn't back down. They broke loose again. The Grim Reaper asked, "So is it guilt that drives you to save her?"

"No," Edward answered, breathing raggedly. "Not guilt. I made a promise."

"A promise?" the Grim Reaper repeated, almost uninterested.

"Yes. That's why I can't give up. I have to win. I made a promise that I would protect her. That I would bring her home. I swore it on my soul!" And Edward leaped at The Grim Reaper with such speed and strength that not even he could see the attack coming. He didn't have to.

The Grim Reaper knew it was all right to lose. He closed his eyes and smiled. "You're strong, Edward Mikes. But the path you've chosen will be the hardest battle of all, for it leads away from the ones you love."

"I already know that. It doesn't change a thing. My soul for hers. That's the way it should be."

It was over so fast that for a moment they just stood there, utterly still. They looked like two friends standing next to each other. But the Grim Reaper's expression was one of shock, and Edward's was one of cold calmness. He heard the gasp of pain and surprise. The Grim Reaper fell to his knees, his scythe falling beside him and then vanishing into a beam of light. It faded up into the sky before disappearing altogether.

Zachary watched it go with a bemused look on his face. "So … it's over. I am the Grim Reaper no longer."

"Yes," Edward answered.

Zachary stared down at the wound across his torso. No blood emerged; he was already dead. But still he was dying now as the Reaper. "Is it okay … for me to die?"

"Yes," Edward said again, staring down at Zachary. "You may rest in peace now, Zachary Connor. The responsibility of the Grim Reaper is my burden to bear."

"Zachary!" They suddenly heard a joyful cry. They both turned as Fate came running toward them. Tears were running down her cheeks as she flung herself at Zachary. She wrapped her arms around his neck and kissed him everywhere on the face. Zach held her close, burying his face in her neck. "You're not cold anymore," Fate said weakly.

"I love you, Fate."

"I love you too, Zach."

"Thank you for waiting for me all this time."

"Don't be silly. As if I could ever move on without you."

They continued to hold each other, never wanting to let each other go again. But finally Zachary looked up to see Edward walking away from them. "Wait, Edward." He waited for Edward to stop and turn back to them before saying hoarsely, "Thank you."

"You're welcome."

"Remember, Edward. The path you walk may be one of darkness—"

"But I'm heading toward the dawn," Edward finished for him.

Zachary nodded and smiled. Fate looked up at Edward too and smiled her thanks.

Edward nodded in kind and said quietly, "It's time to move on. Walk the path. Head north and find peace."

Zachary helped Fate to stand. With Zach's arm around Fate's waist, she waved one last time, and the two of them disappeared to find the rest they longed for together.

Edward turned to the Forget-Me-Not Garden. He had been waiting so long for this, and now he could finally see her again. His dawn was resting inside.

CHAPTER EIGHT

Awake

Emily and Edward

Edward entered the garden. He had never been there before, but he knew exactly where he was going. Knowledge of being the Grim Reaper now rested within him, and all of his powers. He needed no one to show him what to do or where to go. He knew his job well now. Soon he would have to start reaping and guiding the souls. He could sense All Hallows' Eve coming to an end. But none of that mattered now as his eyes finally founded her. She was awake and waiting for him.

Emily still sat on the stone slab where she had slept, but the second Edward became the Grim Reaper, she had woken. Emily stayed where she was. She knew he would come for her. He always did.

Edward saw her first. She was sitting there quietly, staring up at the moon. It was sinking but it still cast a silver-pale light that fell on her upturned face, making it glow. She was as lovely as always.

Edward stopped to stare at her. She sensed he was there and turned to look at him. Her wide, blue-eyed gaze rested on him. There was such joy and love there—and it was just for him.

"Edward," Emily whispered weakly.

"Emily," Edward said as he approached her. "Are you all right?"

"Yes, just feeling a little dizzy," Emily laughed, but her laugh stopped suddenly.

"What's wrong?"

Emily stared at him in horror before stuttering, "Edward! Y-you're covered in wounds. Oh my God! How are you still standing? Are you okay?" She tried to stand up, but she got dizzy from the motion. Edward caught and steadied her. Waking from an eternal slumber took a toll, but she would recover, Edward reasoned, as Emily fretted over his wounds.

"I'm fine. See, look, my wounds are already healing." And they were. The gaping wounds were closing over rapidly. He'd stopped bleeding a while ago, probably when he became the Grim Reaper.

Edward suddenly became aware of Emily's body shaking. He realized to his horror that she was crying. "Emily," he said anxiously, "it's okay."

Emily grasped his shirt tightly. She finally turned her face up to his, tears streaming down her cheeks. "How can you say that? How can you say you are fine? It's not okay. You shouldn't have come for me. Because now …"

Emily started sobbing. Edward simply held her to him, silently giving her the support she needed. She clung to him as if afraid to let go. Finally her sobs stopped and she whispered, "So it's true? What you are now is …"

"The Grim Reaper. It's true."

"You did it to save me. Why, Edward? You could've kept living without me. You could've lived."

"How can you ask me that? As if I would leave you here."

"You've done so much, and all because of me."

"You're here because of me."

"It wasn't your fault."

"Emily," Edward said patiently, waiting for her to look up at him again, "I came because I would do anything to save you. Because I love you."

Emily took a shaky breath before answering, "I love you too, Edward. So much."

For a long while they just stood there, holding each other. Content to be together again. It was all Edward wanted.

Emily tucked her head under his chin and buried her face in his chest. Edward rested his chin on top of her head and breathed in her familiar rain and lavender scent. The moon continued to sink though, and being the Grim Reaper, he could hear the first of the moans from the souls on Dead Man's Path. They were starting to sense they were alone, and they were becoming restless.

"You're so cold," Emily whispered hoarsely as she pressed her body against his, trying to warm it.

"Emily," Edward breathed, and she looked up at him again. Her lips sought his, and he bent to kiss her. She tasted the same too, and he kissed her hungrily, longing for the familiar sensation. He stopped when she started to lose her balance again. Emily protested when he stopped, but he knew it was for the best. Emily wouldn't open her eyes though, and she wouldn't let go of him.

"It's almost dawn."

Emily finally opened her eyes and looked up at him with a panicked expression. "Edward. At dawn you will …"

"Yes. I will have to leave. I can sense the souls becoming restless."

"No," Emily said shakily. "You can't leave me. We can't be apart."

"I will never leave your side, Emily. You have to trust me. I will always be with you."

"I want to stay with you," Emily cried against his chest.

"Think of Dave. He'll be worried about you."

"Life can never be the same without you."

Edward didn't have an answer to that. Emily clung to him, trying to disappear in his very self, never wanting to part from him. Edward would have been content to spend the rest of his life holding her just like this. But time was short.

When Emily opened her eyes, she was still in Edward's arms, but they were sitting on the boulder on top of the hill, where the two of them had watched a hundred sunsets. Only this time, the sun was rising. They didn't talk as the pink clouds turned golden. The air was fresh and cool. Emily shivered as a breeze blew over them. She leaned against him and tucked her head under his chin.

"Edward, what will I tell your mom? What will I say to everyone? How can I keep going without you?"

"It will be all right. Tell my mother that I love her and I will see her again someday."

They fell silent again. Emily willed the sun to freeze, to sink back so that the night could return, so that she could keep Edward with her forever. She dreaded the words she knew he would say. Finally she heard his sigh. "The souls are restless. I have to go."

"No. I don't want you to go."

"I have to, Emily. I can't leave them."

Emily hugged him tightly and whispered, "I know. Will you come back to me?"

"Always," Edward swore solemnly. "I will never leave your side."

It took all of Emily's strength, but she finally made herself let go of him. Edward let go of her too and stood. Emily suddenly realized that he was wearing a long black robe, just like the previous Grim Reaper. He held a massive scythe by his side. All of the wounds he had received in battle were healed. He looked strong, and to Emily, he was the most beautiful thing in the world.

He surprised her when he reached into his robe and pulled out something. He turned to her and took her left hand. Emily could feel the tears running down her cheeks as he put a beautiful pearl ring on her fourth finger. "My heart will always belong to you, Emily Thorn. I will love you until the end of time. I don't know how long it will be, but will you wait for me?"

"You have to ask?" Emily said shakily as she stood too and threw her arms around him. "I will wait for you forever, Edward. There will never be anyone I love more than you. I will love you until the end of time."

"Thank you." Edward smiled at her, emotion suddenly fierce in his eyes. Then he let her go and started walking away.

Emily could feel the panic rising in her chest as she watched him. Suddenly she burst out running toward him and called, "Edward?"

He turned just in time to catch her as she threw herself at him and kissed him with all the passion and love she felt for him. It was like kissing ice. She felt him kiss her back just as fiercely as he crushed her to him. She was breathless when he pulled away. He whispered, "Keep a sharp eye out at sunset."

Emily opened her eyes and she was alone. The sun's warm rays hit her cold skin, and she stood there watching as the sun chased away the last of the darkness. Tears rolled down her face as she touched the pearl ring Edward had given her.

She didn't have long to wait before her father surprised her by pulling up in his truck. The look of pure panic changed into one of relief when Old Dave's eyes settled on his daughter. Of course Edward had known Emily's father wouldn't be at home. He would be out looking for her. And of course he had known where Dave would look next for his missing daughter.

David Thorn got out of his truck and ran to Emily as she collapsed into his arms. "Hey, Emily, it's okay. You're going to be okay. Daddy's got you. It'll be okay." He kept babbling as he held Emily close to his chest. The fear of losing his only child made his knees weak.

"Dad, I'm okay," Emily whispered as tears fell down her cheeks. "I need to see Mrs. Mikes. I have to talk to her." Emily couldn't help the way she cringed when she said Edward's last name.

"Okay, honey. I'll get a hold of Sarah. It'll be okay," David kept saying as he helped Emily to his truck.

The Grim Reaper watched them leave. Emily's world was forever cast in a fading twilight for him. Because all life ended at one point in time. Even this world. Edward watched the love of his life lean weakly against the passenger seat of Old Dave's car as her father tried to talk to her.

Ramona the owl flew to Edward and perched on his shoulder. Her eyes blinked sleepily as the sun rose. It was time to return to the never-ending night of Edward's new world. He looked one last time at Emily before the truck drove out of sight. Soon they would be together again. Until then, he could wait.

The Beginning of Forever

Emily and Edward

Emily didn't know how she finally convinced her father to leave the house for the night. It took a lot of swearing that she would be fine, and even then Emily almost had to shove him out. She guessed she couldn't blame him. After all, she had scared the hell out of him when she didn't return home that night a year ago. When he realized she wasn't coming home, he had spent the night looking for her. Even after he found her, she hadn't given him a reason to think that she was all right. She was a wreck for a while after losing Edward.

The police searched for Edward's missing body for days before ending the search. His mother had a funeral for him. Emily held her the whole time as they both sobbed. Old Dave didn't cry, but he said fiercely, "He was a good man. A man I would have been proud to call son."

Old Dave made Emily promise that she would stay at home for the night, and Emily swore. The carnival was back in town and some of her friends were going, but Emily shuddered at the thought of ever going again.

She had managed to finish high school, but was unsure of what to do with her life. She didn't really care right now. There was only one thing on her mind for tonight. So after one last, worried look at her, Old Dave left to join his friends for an outing at the bar. He hadn't been out much for a long time. Emily really hoped he had a good time, for all the worry that she caused him.

The house was quiet after he left. Emily simply waited. She knew he was coming, because he promised he would. Because he loved her. The pearl ring rested on her finger as a symbol of that promise.

The sun set once again on All Hallows' Eve. Emily watched it sink behind the mountains. When the sun had finally set, she heard a polite knock on the door.

With a wild rush of hope and happiness Emily ran to yank open the door. He was standing there, waiting. As pale and as beautiful as he had been on the day he left. With a cry of joy Emily threw herself into his waiting arms.